"I have never been in danger before."

"An ambulance should be coming with the police any minute now. Can you make it?"

Katie moaned. "I do not know. Can we get down now?"

Adam still hadn't figured out the whereabouts of the shooter. But the alternative, Katie fainting and both of them falling out of the tree, wasn't any better.

"Sure. Let's go." He stepped down a couple of branches and then turned to hold her around the waist and help her down. But with a look of dismay, she stared at her fingers, bloody from her leg wound, her face even whiter than before. He grabbed her around the waist. "Katie?"

Another shot rang out, tearing through the branches around them.

Surely they had been found. That shot had been aimed more directly at Katie.

She stared at him with glassy eyes. Time seemed to stand still in the nanosecond before she closed them.

Then she pitched forward off the branch and plummeted to the ground, her unconscious body pulling him with her.

By sixth grade, **Meghan Carver** knew she wanted to write. After a degree in English from Millikin University, she detoured to law school, completing a Juris Doctor from Indiana University. She then worked in immigration law and taught college-level composition. Now she homeschools her six children with her husband. When she isn't writing, homeschooling or planning another travel adventure, she is active in her church, sews and reads.

Books by Meghan Carver

Love Inspired Suspense

Under Duress
Deadly Disclosure
Amish Country Amnesia
Amish Covert Operation

AMISH COVERT OPERATION

MEGHAN CARVER

HARLEQUIN® LOVE INSPIRED® SUSPENSE

Recycling programs
for this product may
not exist in your area.

 LOVE INSPIRED BOOKS

ISBN-13: 978-1-335-23222-9

Amish Covert Operation

www.Harlequin.com

Printed in U.S.A.

I will bless the Lord at all times:
his praise shall continually be in my mouth.
–Psalms 34:1

To the Amish friends the Lord has brought into my life recently. I am grateful for your kindness and generosity in answering my questions and opening yourselves to me. You know who you are.

ONE

The steady rhythm of the bicycle did little to calm her nerves. Ominous dark blue clouds propelled Katie Schwartz forward. Faster. Her twin girls, Ruth and Rebekah, were safely ensconced with friends, and the adrenaline pulsing through her cemented her resolve to see this through.

A slight breeze ruffled the leaves, sending a few skittering across the road. But then it died, leaving an unnatural stillness in the hush of the oncoming storm. The only things still fluttering were her skirt around her knees and the ties of her prayer *kapp* flying behind her. They tickled her legs and her neck, like ants at a summer picnic, but she didn't dare let loose of the handlebars. Beads of perspiration dotted her forehead.

As she rounded a curve, the blue-black clouds chasing her, her *bruder*'s house and woodworking shop appeared. The white-sided house sat silent, not even the rocking chair on the front porch daring to move. She steered her bicycle around the house and to the barn door.

Should she call out? Announce herself?

What had her *bruder* been up to? What was keeping him from his family, from her and her daughters? It had been two months since she had seen him, and in their tight-knit Amish community, two months seemed like an eternity. Not even the bishop had been able to compel a meeting with him.

She wanted to call out a greeting, but her voice stuck in her throat before she could form the words.

She leaned the bike against the porch railing and stepped silently to the barn door. Her hair prickled on her neck, and she spun around to scan the nearby fields. By midsummer, the corn was tall enough to hide a man. Was someone there? She surveyed the adjoining field and woods, but the stillness revealed no one. Instead it settled on her shoulders like a heavy cloak. Not a bird or a cicada ventured to sing. She couldn't hear any animals scampering around or even automobiles on the nearby road.

She knocked on the door, the sound ricocheting around the silence of the yard, and then it swung open under her knock. Katie stepped inside, pausing to let her eyes adjust to the dim interior.

"Timothy?"

The volume of her own voice startled her in the eerie quiet. Yellow light from outside filtered through the rafters, and she closed the door behind her. She rubbed her forearms, but the goose bumps persisted.

A horse snickered from the stall. Wherever Timothy had gone, it wasn't far enough to take his horse and buggy. The sound of hay scraping on the floor sifted through the quiet, followed by a scurrying sound. She grasped her skirt. Her *bruder* needed a cat who was a better mouser.

Before she could reach the door to the workshop, the sound of a steady pounding reached her. Or was it footsteps?

"Timothy?" But anxiety's stranglehold on her throat made it come out as a weak squeak.

She clutched her apron in her damp palms as she inched closer to the door. Lightning suddenly flashed through the window, illuminating the stall, the animal and a pair of black shoes peeking out from under the bottom board. A fistful of hay flew in her direction. She pulled her arms up to protect herself, desperate to stifle a sneeze that tickled her nose. Thunder crashed a split second later, at the same time as the clatter of the back door.

The next moment, all was still again.

Katie rushed to the woodworking room and thrust the door closed. She leaned against it, gulping deep breaths to steady herself, clutching the neck of her dress, her eyes closed in a vain attempt to calm herself. Gradually her heartbeat returned to a rhythm that felt almost normal, and she loosened her grip on the smooth fabric.

She slowly opened her eyes. A small, rectangular piece of paper was staring back at her from the floor near the workbench. As she bent to pick it up, another flash of lightning struck, making the words on the front of the card clearly visible. *SOCIAL SECURITY* arched in capital letters across the top. The name on the paper was one she didn't know, and underneath were nine numbers that were meaningless to her.

She had heard of several *Englisch* laws from which

the Amish were exempt. Social security was one of them. Their Amish faith forbade insurance, which was what their bishops said the government program was. So if they weren't going to benefit from it, they didn't have to pay into it. She had never had a card that looked like that, and she was fairly certain that her *bruder* had never had a card like that either. So why was this little piece of paper here, in his woodworking shop?

Another crash of thunder shook the barn, but this time it was paired with a crash from within the barn, as well. Katie jumped back against the door, her fingers releasing the little bit of card. It fluttered to the floor, and she grabbed the knob, jerked the door open, and rushed to the exterior door. She grabbed her bicycle from the side porch of the house, unwilling to stick around and find out who was there.

The memory of the hunting cabin in the woods rose up in her mind as she pedaled hard down the asphalt road. She felt desperate to talk to her *bruder*, her abdomen clenching from the exertion and a fair dose of fear. The bishop was kind and caring, and Sarah was a *gut* friend. But there was nothing like family, and with both their parents gone, he was all she had. Perhaps he would be at the cabin they had played in as children. Sometimes Amish woodworkers harvested their own lumber for special projects. In the past, Timothy had also spent a fair share of time there sketching new furniture designs.

A few days ago, some of the Amish teens from her church district had told her that they had seen something suspicious in the woods, but whoever or whatever it had been had disappeared before they could catch up.

They thought perhaps it had been hunters, but deer season didn't start until November.

A fresh ache coursed through her with longing for her husband. If only he were here with her, he could talk to Timothy. Find out what was wrong. Help restore her brother's relationship with *Gott* and with his sister and nieces. Of course he would have protected her, too. But she had been tougher than he had realized. Or had that toughness emerged out of necessity and desperation in these last two years since his death?

She pedaled hard into the afternoon's yellow stillness, replaying the events of the past few months. Timothy had begun acting strangely not long after her husband was killed. A tear coursed down her cheek, and she removed a hand from the handlebars just long enough to swipe it away. Wasn't life difficult enough already without her husband? That aloneness had been a new sensation and one to which she still hadn't grown accustomed. But to also lose her *bruder*, her only remaining family apart from her girls, with his odd behavior? It seemed more than she could bear.

A dirt road veered off the pavement to the right, and with just a few more minutes of concentrated pedaling and praying, she came within view of the cabin. It seemed safer, somehow, to leave the bicycle propped against a tree, where it would be out of sight. From a position where she was concealed behind a bush, she surveyed the area. The eerie stillness had followed her from her *bruder*'s property, a yellowish haze of the impending storm permeating the clearing. But no one was in sight, and even the squirrels had ceased their chattering.

With a deep inhalation of the scent of pine trees and summer soil, she stepped into the clearing, keeping to the edge until the last moment. Eight paces brought her to the corner of the structure, where she grabbed a wooden crate and placed it in front of a window.

Gingerly she stepped up, clutching her full skirt in one hand and the window trim in the other. Through her shoes, her toes gripped the edge of the rickety crate. Desperation to stay upright and not teeter off sent a surge of adrenaline coursing through her as she swiped a hand across the grimy window of the hunter's shack. The crate dipped, and Katie grasped the frame of the window again. A splinter of wood pierced her skin, the sting of penetration barely registering as she focused on the task at hand.

"Timothy?" she whispered to herself. "Where are you?"

The boys who lived on the other side of the woods had to be right. They had told her they had seen Timothy going into an old shack in the woods, their description matching this one exactly. It had been months since she had seen her brother, and many more months since that day that had made her a widow and changed the course of their family, but it hadn't even been a week since she had cried herself to sleep. Even now the familiar tears threatened to blur her vision.

With the crate stabilized, she swiped over the glass again and squinted inside. But all that stared back at her was more grime. *Ach*, if only she weren't so short! But at a mere five feet four inches, she knew she needed a step stool for nearly every endeavor, especially for an old cabin elevated on cement blocks and with tiny windows. A bee buzzed around her face, and she waved a hand to shoo it away. The crate tipped again, and she grabbed at the window trim before she could tumble off.

Movement inside snagged her attention, although she couldn't make out figures. It was like looking through the bottom of a glass bottle, with only large blobs moving around. Voices filtered through the window, one louder than the other. What was going on in there? And was Timothy involved?

"*Gott*, help!" The whispered prayer flew from her lips heavenward. "Restore Timothy to the only family he has left!" He needed love and rest and plenty of good, nutritious food. He needed the strength within the Amish community, the salvation in Jesus Christ that the bishop preached and the productive life of a man of faith who worked with his hands. He needed family, a cornerstone of any Amish person's life.

Her nose touched the glass in her efforts to see inside. A face suddenly appeared in the window. It was distorted by the cracks in the glass, but it appeared to be her *bruder*. A moment later, the face disappeared.

She jumped from the crate and headed toward the corner of the cabin. Now that he had seen her, he had to come out and explain himself and return with her, stopping whatever this clandestine meeting was all about. Yet despite the warm summer air, a chill crept up her arms as she rounded the corner. The sour scent of the humidity in the woods tingled her nose and seeped into her brain, beginning the light pulse of a coming headache. Was she relieved that she had found him? Or was she apprehensive of who he was with and what he was doing? The emotions warred within her.

A man dressed in plain clothing, homespun pants and a light blue shirt stepped out through the door.

"Timothy!" But the wild look in his eyes stopped her from speaking further.

And then she saw it. A gun was pressed into his back. But the man with the weapon didn't step out.

"Katie! Run! Go!"

She jerked backward, an instinctual reaction to the presence of the deadly weapon. Panic gripped her throat, her mouth suddenly chalky. What should she do? Could she help him? But there was no way she was going to advance any closer to the door and that gun.

"*Dabber schpring!* Run quickly!"

She stepped backward, her gaze trained on the weapon. With another step, she saw her *bruder* pulled back inside the cabin. The gun reemerged, and she turned to run.

She was five steps away when the weapon fired, an explosive sound that hurt her ears. She pushed herself farther and faster, but her legs were burning. It seemed to take too many steps to reach the tree line. Voices sounded behind her, louder and harsher, as if they were exiting the cabin. She hiked up her skirt, desperately grabbing at the fabric with her sweaty palms, and crouched low as she continued to run.

Another explosion fired nearby, and a sapling splintered to her right. How close was the shooter? Was he following her? She glanced back over her shoulder to check his position, and her foot caught on something. Air rushed past her as she fell face-first into the leaves and dirt.

The ground slammed into her midsection, forcing

the air out of her lungs. As she fought to get a breath, a hand clamped onto her shoulder. She struggled to turn over, but all she could see out of her peripheral vision was what she assumed was the man's other hand. He held a gun.

That was it, then. This would be the end.

"Are you all right?" Adam Troyer kept his voice to a low whisper. He glanced back to check the position of the men who had been in the cabin. The one with the weapon continued to advance. Whoever this Amish woman was, he needed to get her out of there. "Can you breathe? Can you run?"

Her answer was a scream.

Oh, that wasn't good. "Shh, shh. I'm not with them. I'm law enforcement." Another shot struck a nearby tree. "Come with me if you want to live."

The screaming stopped as he grasped her upper arm and pulled her to her feet. She grimaced, but if they didn't hurry, they might both be killed. He broke into a jog, the woman running alongside him, trying to brush dirt and leaves off her skirt with one hand and holding on to her *kapp* with the other.

"Danki." The thank-you puffed out with a breath as they hurried further into the woods.

He nodded his acknowledgment. She certainly sounded like a real Amish woman, but was she? It could be that she practiced the accent. Was she an innocent bystander? Or was she in league with whoever was in the cabin, just dressed to look Amish so as not to attract attention?

The sounds of their pursuer crashing through the

underbrush grew louder. They would never be able to get away, especially with this woman encumbered by her full skirt and *kapp*. It was time for concealment.

Adam pulled her toward a thick stand of poplar trees. "I called nine-one-one. It's the fastest way to get reinforcements here. Right now we need to hide."

She nodded and stepped in front of him as quickly as she could, a look of panic mingled with determination etching fine lines around her eyes. Scanning the forest growth around them, she whispered without looking back, "We go up."

It was brilliant. From a tree, not only would they be hidden but he could survey the area and, hopefully, find the man who had chased them from the cabin. A few more steps took them to the base of a thick tree with low-hanging branches.

"Here?"

Katie nodded. "Not for long, I pray."

But by the time he had holstered his weapon and cupped his hands together to provide a step up for her, she had gathered her skirt tightly around her legs with one hand. With the other, she grasped an upper branch. In a few seconds, she was several feet up the tree. Apparently climbing trees was not a new activity for her.

Adam followed behind until they came to a spot where two thick branches ran parallel and provided a sort of bench for them. He settled her in the seat and then lowered himself beside her. Branches full with leaves fanned around them, so thick that he had to pull a branch aside to be able to peek out. This would do well.

He couldn't see anyone below, but that didn't mean it was safe to emerge from their hiding spot. He turned to the Amish woman, her face startlingly close to his in their tight surroundings. "I'm Adam Troyer, by the way." He kept his voice to a whisper. "Immigration and Customs Enforcement special agent."

She turned to him. "Katie Schwartz." Her dark blue eyes flashed in the dimness of their cover as she pierced him with her gaze. "What are you doing here?"

Wait a minute. He was the one who should ask the questions. "Surveillance." He would answer that one, though, hopefully to build rapport, and then fire his questions at her. From his position earlier, he had seen her approach the cabin, acting suspicious and watching over her shoulder. Yes, she looked Amish. Even sounded Amish. But he had no way of knowing, at this point in time, that she actually was Amish. What if she was part of the criminal ring he was seeking, perhaps sent out for an errand, innocent-looking in her Amish garb, and now she was returning? He would stick close to her until he knew for sure who she was. In the meantime, though, there was no harm in her knowing he was ICE. He would not tell her any more.

"I heard a man in the cabin tell you to run away. Why are you here?" He peeked through the leaves again. Still no one had approached the tree. This was not the time or place to question her, but he could gather a little bit of information. If she was one of them, then she would be arrested. If she wasn't, then perhaps she had some insider information that would be helpful to the investigation. So much about her seemed suspicious and made the hair on the back of his hands raise up.

"I am looking for *mein bruder.*" She scrunched her eyes and rubbed at them, a tear squeezing out and run-

ning down her cheek. She sniffed, a sound too loud for
their concealed location.

A crashing sounded somewhere below, and Adam
parted the branches to see the man with the weapon
several yards off. He was looking straight ahead, and
Adam couldn't see his face, only the top of his head,
which was covered with a baseball cap.

Katie sniffed again, and Adam raised his finger to
his lips to shush her.

"Allergies," she whispered. She wrinkled her nose
and held a finger underneath.

Oh, no. This wouldn't help at all.

In a split second, she tilted her head back as if a
sneeze was imminent. Adam grabbed her with both
arms and, with his hand on the back of her head, pulled
her into his shoulder. Her sneeze was muffled in his
shirt, but she instantly pushed away from him. He cast
what he hoped was an apologetic look in her direction
and shrugged his shoulders, but he didn't dare speak.
A peek between the branches revealed that their hiding
space remained secure.

Without knowing how many men were in the cabin
or how much firepower they had, he couldn't take them
on all by himself. It was very likely he was outmanned
and outgunned, and the best thing to do was wait for
local law enforcement to show up. Still, despite the
softness of the Amish woman next to him, or perhaps
because of it, the hiding place was growing more uncomfortable by the second.

The woman sniffled again, and he pulled her into
his shoulder as the second sneeze erupted. He wanted
to shush her, but sneezes were uncontrollable. It wasn't

her fault. Plus he didn't want the man somewhere below to hear him. They were like sitting ducks up here in their perch.

As the shuddering of the sneeze subsided, Katie pushed away. She seemed as uncomfortable as he was. But her push must have been too hard, for she wobbled on the branch, her hands grasping for anything to keep her steady. She finally found traction with one hand on the branch and one hand on his arm. Once settled, she let go and straightened her *kapp* and her skirt.

"*Danki.* You have saved me two times."

Before he could whisper his response, the tree trunk exploded next to him.

"*Ach!*" Katie cried, her hand flying to her leg, obviously in pain but still trying to keep quiet.

Instincts kicked in, and he grabbed her close and pulled her down, trying to shield her from any other gunshots. Did the shooter know where they were, or was he the type to shoot randomly? Adam peered through the branches, but he couldn't see a thing.

"Are you hit?" he whispered, but he knew the answer already.

Katie drew her hand away from her leg. There was blood on it. "Is that what has happened? My leg burns terribly." Tears sprang to her eyes as she clutched the spot on her leg.

"Let me see." After one more look through the branches, he gently removed her hand from the spot and separated the folds of her skirt. The fabric was torn and bloody around the edges, but the injury was not bleeding profusely. She whimpered in pain as he touched the spot and then gathered the folds of her skirt to apply direct pressure to the wound. "Hold this here. We have to get out of here."

But was it safe to descend? He gingerly pulled the branches apart, but he couldn't see anyone. A squirrel chattered nearby. Could that have been what drew the attention of the shooter? At least there hadn't been another shot. Could Katie wait until law enforcement arrived? If they left the tree now, they could put themselves directly in the path of the shooter.

As Katie applied the pressure, her face grew pale, a sheen of perspiration breaking out over her forehead. "I have never been in danger before."

Suddenly she didn't look steady enough to sit on the branches. "An ambulance should be coming with the police any minute now. Can you make it?"

She moaned and clutched her stomach. "I do not know. Can we get down now?"

It wasn't the best idea, considering he still hadn't figured out the whereabouts of the shooter. But the alternative, Katie fainting and both of them falling out of the tree, wasn't any better. Down it would be.

"Sure. Let's go." He stepped down a couple of branches and then turned to hold her around the waist and help her down. They stairstepped down to the bottom branch before a loud rustling sounded from brush nearby.

His heart thrust itself against his chest, and he turned back to signal Katie to be quiet. But with a look of dismay, she stared at her fingers, bloody from her leg wound, her face even whiter than before. He grabbed her around the waist. "Katie?"

Another shot rang out, tearing through the branches around them.

Surely they had been found. That shot had been aimed more directly at Katie.

She stared at him with glassy eyes. Time seemed to stand still in the nanosecond before she closed them. Then she pitched forward, off the branch, and plummeted to the ground, her lifeless body pulling him with her.

TWO

The pierce of sirens slowly circled in her mind as she became aware of the trees, the clouds and even the ground spinning around her. She grasped for something to steady herself with so that she wouldn't fall off. But off what? Where was she?

The sirens stopped, and the buzz of summer insects filled the silence. Something tickled her forehead, and with great effort, she lifted a hand to brush it away.

"Katie?"

Whatever was tickling her sprang back, and she brushed it away again.

"Katie, can you open your eyes?"

It was a low but strong male voice, and she forced her eyes open to find that this man was the one tickling her forehead, brushing and smoothing her hair away with his hand. She closed her eyes again, wanting to lie there and rest. But the man squeezed her shoulder. "Katie, you fainted. Can you wake up? Are you all right?"

Adam. That was his name. The events of the afternoon came rushing back—looking for her *bruder*,

hair knot

on the co

faith in he

As Ad

bulance, t

taking he

asking a

solution s

in the veh

first bull

where clo

skimmed

dage the

so, but the

them, you

drugstore

"Praise

for a quick

she popp

with eyes

Adam

bulance, t

He dug ou

of the stic

With a

daged her

probably

heal up w

"Did I

"Yes. I

the sight

Another shot rang out, tearing through the branches around them.

Surely they had been found. That shot had been aimed more directly at Katie.

She stared at him with glassy eyes. Time seemed to stand still in the nanosecond before she closed them. Then she pitched forward, off the branch, and plummeted to the ground, her lifeless body pulling him with her.

TWO

The pierce of sirens slowly circled in her mind as she became aware of the trees, the clouds and even the ground spinning around her. She grasped for something to steady herself with so that she wouldn't fall off. But off what? Where was she?

The sirens stopped, and the buzz of summer insects filled the silence. Something tickled her forehead, and with great effort, she lifted a hand to brush it away.

"Katie?"

Whatever was tickling her sprang back, and she brushed it away again.

"Katie, can you open your eyes?"

It was a low but strong male voice, and she forced her eyes open to find that this man was the one tickling her forehead, brushing and smoothing her hair away with his hand. She closed her eyes again, wanting to lie there and rest. But the man squeezed her shoulder. "Katie, you fainted. Can you wake up? Are you all right?"

Adam. That was his name. The events of the afternoon came rushing back—looking for her *bruder*, finding him at the cabin, climbing the tree with the ICE special agent.

Her head rested on a soft surface, and she noticed he now wore only a navy T-shirt with his khaki cargo pants. His button-down shirt was gone. He must have used it as a pillow for her.

Where is Timothy? With her abdominal muscles, she pulled herself to a sitting position. The sky and trees began a violent spin around her, and she swayed against Adam. With eyes closed, she leaned against him until the spinning subsided.

Slowly she opened her eyes. "Are we safe now?"

"Yes. The police are here. They found the cabin cleared out."

"*Mein bruder?* Timothy?"

"I'm not sure who your brother is, but everyone was gone. I would guess they scattered when they heard the sirens."

"Who are they? What are they doing here?"

"First let's get you some medical care. The paramedics are here. Can you make it to the ambulance? They drove off the country road and into the grass, but they're going to have a tough time getting through the trees to us." He scanned the horizon behind her.

"*Jah*, I think so. But will you stay close? Just in case?" It felt like a weak smile that she offered him, but he smiled in return, a kind look in his eyes that hadn't been there before.

It seemed a long way through the trees to the spot where the ambulance had pulled up into the clearing. Katie breathed with relief to see that the paramedic was a woman. She looked barely older than Katie, with dark hair knotted into a bun. As she helped Katie lie down on the cot, she smiled warmly, and Katie had instant faith in her.

As Adam leaned against the open door of the ambulance, the paramedic quickly assessed the situation, taking her temperature and blood pressure, as well as asking a dozen or more questions. Then she removed solutions and bandages from various bins and boxes in the vehicle. "Special Agent Troyer was correct. The first bullet grazed your outer thigh. It didn't go anywhere close to your femur, your upper leg bone. It just skimmed the soft tissue, so I'm going to clean and bandage the wound. You might be hobbling for a week or so, but there won't be any lasting effects. If you need them, you can buy crutches or a cane from any local drugstore."

"Praise *Gott* for His protection." She closed her eyes for a quick prayer, but when the darkness began to spin, she popped them open again. *Gott* would hear prayers with eyes open, as well.

Adam had stepped away from the door of the ambulance, but he soon returned with a long, stout stick. He dug out a pocketknife and began whittling one end of the stick.

With a gentle touch, the paramedic cleaned and bandaged her forehead. "You have some minor abrasions, probably from your fall from the tree. They will also heal up with time. I don't expect you to have any scars."

"Did I faint? Is that why I am so dizzy?"

"Yes. It's called vasovagal syncope. Do you faint at the sight of blood?" She nodded toward Adam. "Special Agent Troyer told me you found your injury first by the blood on your skirt."

Katie glanced at Adam, but he was studying his stick. Surely he was listening. "*Nein*. Not that I know of. When one of my twins scrapes a knee, I do not like that she is hurt, but the blood does not bother me."

"Extreme emotional distress is probably your trigger then. You've been shot at twice. That makes for a difficult afternoon. In response, your heart rate slowed and your blood pressure dropped. That made you faint."

The paramedic made it sound so matter-of-fact, but that was her job. Still Katie pressed the back of her hand to her forehead, an effort to wipe away the stickiness of anxiety.

"Would you like to go to the hospital? They can do a more thorough examination there."

"Do I need to?"

"Not necessarily. It's completely up to you."

Concern for her *bruder* was pushed aside by thoughts of her twins. The sun was slanting lower and lower, and the four-year-old girls must be anxious for her return. Her friend Sarah would take *gut* care of them, feeding them supper and probably too many treats. But Katie didn't like to be away too long. A mother needed to be with her children, and children needed to be with their mother. A trip to the hospital would most likely extend into the nighttime hours.

"*Danki*, but *nein*. I am sure I will be fine with some rest." How much would an ambulance cost, anyway? For sure and for certain, it was expensive, a cost with which she did not want to burden the community.

"I'll take you home." Adam looked up from his whittling. It wasn't even a question. It was a statement, and a shiver stairstepped down Katie's spine. Was it from the richness of his baritone voice or the insinuation that he had more questions for her?

An hour later, with the help of the paramedic, Katie scooted off the cot. A strong twinge of pain shot up her leg from the site of the wound. In the couple of steps toward the ambulance door, though, she determined that she could make it. But Special Agent Troyer was there with hand outstretched, and she willingly leaned most of her weight on him to get out of the vehicle.

Once both of her feet were firmly planted on the ground, Adam held the stick out to her. "It's a rough job since I didn't have much time, but I think it will serve its purpose." His voice sounded apologetic.

She took the walking stick from him and touched the simple spiral handle he had whittled at the top. It fit in her hand perfectly. Without letting go of his arm, she leaned into the cane. It held her weight comfortably. "*Danki.* You have skill. That is *gut.*"

Between the cane and Adam's arm, she hobbled to his vehicle, a large black monster of an SUV called a Tahoe. The Amish Taxi that she used was a simple minivan. She had traveled in a van that had carried fourteen of them from their community in Northern Indiana for shopping in Fort Wayne several years ago. Most likely, vehicles like this had passed her buggy many times on the roads, but she had never noticed. Why would she when she had little use for or interest in cars?

"I'll get your bicycle." He left her leaning against the side of the vehicle, retrieved her bicycle from the trees and loaded it into the back. Without breaking a sweat, he returned to her.

At the door, she stared up at the seat. *Ach*, how would she ever get up that high?

As if he had read her thoughts, Adam leaned in and pointed. "Lean on me to get your good leg on the running board. I'll help you up."

A moment later, with Adam lifting on her elbow, she was perched in the SUV. Adam jogged around the front and quickly seated himself behind the wheel. He didn't start the vehicle, though, but turned to her with his eyebrows scrunched into a questioning look.

Apparently he wasn't just going to take her home. She would have to answer more questions first. Her heart thrummed within her chest.

"Why don't you tell me about your brother. What's his name? When did you last see him?" He tapped one finger against the steering wheel.

From this height and location, she had a clear view of the cabin. Several officers were working at various tasks, including one putting yellow tape around the perimeter. What *had* Timothy been doing there? She couldn't imagine, but it hadn't involved sketching.

She closed her eyes and took a deep breath, but everything began to spin. With her eyes open, it wasn't much better. Anxiety overwhelmed her, and her hands began to shake in her lap. Her brother was still out of contact, she sat in the vehicle of a law enforcement officer who had saved her from two bullets and she wasn't sure when she would see her twins again. She grasped one hand with the other, an act of will to stop the trembling, but it only worsened until tears cascaded down her face. She swiped at her cheeks, desperate to get some control over her emotions and be strong for her daughters, but it felt hopeless. Her parents were gone, her husband had been killed two years ago and now she seemed to have lost her *bruder*, as well.

Was she in custody? What were the intentions of this agent? When would she get to Jed and Sarah's house to see her twin girls again? With no husband to step in for her, she would have to have a special reliance on the care of *Gott*. Her leg throbbed, and although the officer was kind enough to make a cane, how would she keep up with the household chores?

Her world was crashing down, and she had no family to which to turn.

The Amish woman sucked in a deep breath and let it out slowly, lifting a dainty finger to wipe away a stray tear.

She was lovely, wholesome, innocent-looking. But Adam couldn't let that influence him. Until he found out exactly what she was doing there and confirmed it with someone reputable, he would consider her a person of interest.

He shifted in his seat to get a better look at her. As he waited for her to begin answering his questions, he noted her light green dress with the white apron, which was soiled from the tree and the shooting. Her dark blond hair was pulled back into a bun, but her *kapp* now sat askew.

Stray thoughts wandered unbidden through his mind. Where would he be right now if his own father hadn't rejected his Amish upbringing? Adam knew a little of the Amish from his infrequent visits to his grandparents, but the faith and lifestyle he had seen in them hadn't saved them from difficult circumstances, including outright rejection and scorn from their own son, Adam's father.

He shook his head to force himself back to the present task, a responsibility that had nothing to do with his own Amish heritage, a generation removed.

Katie stared out the front window, not blinking, and said, "*Mein bruder* is Timothy Schwartz."

Okay, that was a start. Silence stretched between them, but Adam could sit for as long as it took.

"I last saw him on Easter. I do not know where he is or what he has been doing. That is why I was looking for him today." She paused, but he waited patiently. "I found a social security card in his shop, but I do not know the name on it."

Adam hid his surprise. He tucked that valuable piece of information away for later examination as he quickly completed a mental calculation. "So, it's been over two months since you talked to your brother. Isn't that unusual for the Amish? Unless you don't live near here?"

"*Jah*, it is quite unusual. Since I am widowed, I was accustomed to seeing him every day, when he would come to care for my animals. I live close by. I have looked for him many times at his house, but this is the first I came to this cabin." She gestured toward the back of the SUV, where her bike rested. "One person can travel only so far by bicycle."

"Do you ride your bike often?" He felt his eyes narrowing into what felt like his customary expression during interrogations, and he quickly forced what he hoped was simply an inquisitive look. He knew from his grandparents that the Amish were not fond of law enforcement, and he didn't want her to stop talking. At least not until he had all the information he needed.

"*Jah*, it is easier sometimes than hitching up Molly, my horse. I live over on Five Pines Road, a couple of miles from here."

"How long have you lived in Northern Indiana?"

"All my life."

"And you said you were widowed? What about other family?"

"*Nein*. My *daed* and *mamm* died about three years ago, just a few days apart. *Daed* died of a massive heart attack, quite suddenly. A few days later, *Mamm* died of a broken heart. That is what the doctor said." She took a deep breath and stared out the side window, seeming to refocus. "My husband was killed in an accident at work. That was two years ago. Now I only have my twin girls, Ruth and Rebekah. They are four."

"Where are your twins now?"

"They are with my friend Sarah and her husband, Jed. I left them for a little while so I could go to *mein bruder*'s house. I needed to talk to him. To find out what struggle keeps him from his family and the church."

He studied her profile, the drooping prayer *kapp*, the hair that had escaped and now trailed across her cheek, the fine lines around her eyes. She looked tired, exhausted even. Everything she said seemed genuine, and Adam relaxed in his seat ever so slightly. She may not be in cahoots with the shooter, but she still might be a helpful source of information. "Tell me about Sarah and Jed. Who are they, and how do you know them?"

"Sarah has been a *gut* friend since she moved here from Lancaster County several years ago. She was a widow also and had a little girl, and we would help each other out. A few months ago, she married Jedediah Miller. He used to be a police officer from Fort Wayne, but now he is Amish. He works at the same sawmill where my husband did."

He felt a muscle spasm in his jaw, the same one that ticked when he was trying to figure out a case, and he rubbed to soothe it. "If he's Amish, then there's no way I could call him. Or does your church allow telephones?"

"*Nein*. There is a phone shanty not far from their house, but if you are taking me home, you can meet him. I need to pick up my twins, if you are willing."

"Fine. I need to check in with the sheriff, and then we'll be on our way."

He slipped out of the car and closed the door gently, so as not to shake her up further. Katie seemed to be made of tough stuff, but everyone had a limit to their endurance. The slamming of the heavy car door would only add to her jitteriness.

The scene in and around the cabin was intense and busy, but that was the way Adam liked his work. He leaned against the driver's side door and pulled his pocketknife and a small piece of wood out of his pocket. Whittling helped him think, and right now he especially needed to concentrate. A ring of smugglers out of Chicago had expanded, ICE believed, toward Cincinnati. That would take them right through the Amish communities of Northern Indiana. He hadn't had much success in his investigation thus far, and now this Amish woman landed right in the middle. What should he think about it? Where did she fit?

"Troyer!" Sheriff Moore, a man with a thick torso and a jovial demeanor, sauntered toward him. The sheriff's easygoing attitude seemed to be appreciated by the Amish, who apparently had had some difficulty with their last sheriff, but he was a little too laid-back for Adam's preference. Still, the man was well-liked and got the job done. "Find out anything?" He nodded his head toward Katie in the SUV.

"Not much. You know her?" Adam took a few steps toward the sheriff as he scraped his knife over the little piece of wood. It would soon be a squirrel, a twin to the one that already resided in his pocket.

"No. Haven't met her yet."

"She says she's friends with a Sarah and Jedediah Miller. Says Jed's former law enforcement from Fort Wayne."

"Yeah, he's out of it now. Decided he wanted the plain life."

"How'd he end up Amish?" Adam could appreciate a lack of complication as much as the next guy, but leaving electricity behind seemed a little drastic. Why couldn't he just have a sticky bun with his Saturday-morning coffee and old-fashioned newspaper?

"From what I've heard, he was working undercover and about to testify against a ring of counterfeiters when he was found out. Had a snowmobile accident, hit his head on a rock and woke up with amnesia. Sarah found him and took care of him. He's fine now. A real upstanding guy." The sheriff swiped a hand across his brow and adjusted his hat.

The more he heard, the more Adam thought Katie's story was legitimate. There didn't seem to be any other way to explain her presence at the cabin. If her brother was involved in whatever nefarious activity was occurring in the area, she could be a helpful asset. She certainly seemed concerned enough about her brother, despite his wayward ways. He had to take her home anyway, so he'd have a few words with this Jed.

Adam nodded back toward his SUV. "The bullet grazed her leg, so she won't be riding her bike anytime soon. I'll take her to her friends' house to pick up her twins and see if I can get a private word with Jed."

"He'll tell you what he can." The sheriff plucked a long piece of foxtail grass and stuck the stem between his teeth.

"Good. I'd appreciate being kept in the loop with what you find here."

"We don't hope for much. So far we've pulled a bullet out of a tree trunk. We'll look for a match, but I'm doubtful at being able to find the weapon. I'll keep in touch."

"Thanks." Adam turned back to the Tahoe, determined to get a little more of Katie's story from another law enforcement officer, even if he was Amish now.

THREE

As the crow flies, the drive would probably have been only a few minutes, and that certainly would have been safer. But the back roads through the hills and hollows of Northern Indiana Amish country took a bit more of a winding route. Adam found he couldn't get over thirty miles per hour in most stretches. Slowing down for a couple of buggies didn't help either.

The painfully slow speed also didn't help his anxiety at the shooter still being on the loose. Would he come back for Katie? Why was he shooting at her in the first place? Would he go after a law enforcement officer? Some criminals did, and some didn't. Adam just didn't know enough about who this shooter might be to be able to determine his probable next move.

He tore his attention from the rearview mirror and checked both side mirrors. Through the drive, all had been clear. As he crested a hill, an Amish homestead came into view.

"There. On the right." Katie leaned forward as if it would help her get to her children faster, her hand on the cane.

The property wasn't large, but the whitewashed house was sizeable, the barn a cheerful red. Colorful flowers—marigolds, maybe—dotted the edge of the house and the barn. A large vegetable garden filled a back corner. As he approached, a malamute bounded forward, tail wagging and tongue lolling.

Memories of childhood time spent with Amish grandparents struggled to free themselves from the dusty corners of his mind. His *grossmammi* with a plate full of oatmeal cookies and a pitcher of warm milk that was fresh from their dairy cow. His *grossdaadi* sitting on the porch, showing him the finer points of whittling, while his cousins swung from the hayloft. Adam swallowed hard and shoved the memories back to their places. His father's *rumspringa* and continuing alcoholism had altered not only his father's life but the lives of his future children, as well. And after his father's and brother's untimely deaths in the automobile accident, those remembrances didn't deserve the freedom to roam unhindered through his thoughts. The only way to assuage the grief was to maintain his laser-like focus on his job and the justice for victims that he sought every day.

Adam pulled into the lane, and a man emerged from the house, placing a straw hat on his head as he approached the vehicle. Adam opened the car door and hopped out. He smiled as warmly as he could and raised a hand in greeting, palm open and facing out, as he jogged around the front of the Tahoe. The man's countenance was expressionless until Adam helped Katie down from the SUV. As she emerged from behind the door, a wide smile split the man's face, and a woman with three girls, all in identical blue Amish dresses and white starched prayer *kapps*, stepped out of the house.

"Katie, are you all right?"

"*Jah*, Jed." She leaned heavily on Adam's forearm. Grasping the cane, she stepped toward Jed but still held on to Adam's arm.

The woman who must have been Sarah flew toward them. The three girls followed on her heels, all chattering at once.

"*Ach*, Katie! Where have you been? You are injured!"

"*Mamm!* Are you all right?"

"What happened, *Mamm*?"

Sarah frowned in Adam's direction and took Katie's arm from him as twin girls threw their arms around Katie's waist. Both had the same shade of dark blond hair and the same pert nose, although one appeared to have a few more freckles than the other. *Adorable* seemed too blasé of a word to describe them.

"*Liebchen!* My loves!" Katie smiled broadly and shrugged at Adam as she tried to hug both twins with Sarah hanging on. "I will be fine, Sarah. I will tell you everything inside."

He felt himself begin to trust her a little bit more as he observed Katie's affection for her girls. She gently pulled her arm from Sarah, and, leaning on the cane, she tucked a stray hair back into one girl's *kapp* and then ran her finger down the cheek of the other girl. A smile played about her lips as she seemed to relax. With a reflex honed from training and experience, Adam glanced around the yard and down the lane to make sure all was quiet. Then he stepped toward Jed.

"You must be Jedediah Miller. Sheriff Moore told me

you're retired from Fort Wayne PD." He extended his hand, and they shook. "I'm Adam Troyer, special agent with Immigration and Customs Enforcement, Homeland Security."

"Call me Jed. And yes, retired police officer."

Adam felt his eyebrows scrunch together. "You don't sound Amish, like Katie and Sarah."

Jed smiled. "No. Most of my growing-up was in the *Englisch* world. I just took my vows to join the Amish church a few months ago, so I'm still learning. I imagine it'll be a lifelong process." He looked Adam up and down, the smile sliding off his face. "What's your business here?"

Before Adam could respond, Sarah called from the house. Jed turned to wave and then spun back to Adam. "Before you can answer that, we're required to head in the house for cookies and coffee. Or tea. Or milk. Whatever's your pleasure. It's the Amish way."

In the house, Adam squeezed into a place at the long table and gobbled down three of the most delicious oatmeal cookies he had ever eaten. A twin leaned on either side of Katie as she told of going to her brother's house and then to the cabin. All eyes widened at the mention of the gunman, and Jed nodded an acknowledgment to Adam.

"You must leave Ruth and Rebekah here overnight, then." Sarah leaned forward to run a hand down Katie's arm. "You will rest better."

Katie paused before answering. "*Danki.* That would probably be best for my recovery."

As he reached for a fourth cookie, Adam's phone rang, the ringtone a loud gong in the quiet Amish house.

"Excuse me," he said softly and stepped outside the back door before answering.

The late afternoon sun was beginning to cast sleepy shadows across the property, shadows that, to Adam's way of thinking, could hold danger. But Sheriff Moore's voice filled his ear, and the best he could do was visually survey the perimeter.

"Yeah, Troyer? We got nothing. You said you wanted to be kept in the loop, but there's nothin' there. We pulled the bullet from the tree."

"I knew that before I left the site."

"Yeah, and there was nothing worth fingerprinting inside the cabin. Pretty bare in there. All rough wood surfaces, way too porous and too recessed to collect fingerprints. Even if I could find a print, it wouldn't stick to the lift tape. There's no way to lift a print in a wooden cabin."

"So, we got nothing."

"That's what I said."

The door closed behind him, and Adam turned to see Jed step outside. "Thanks anyway, Sheriff." He pocketed his phone.

"Sheriff Moore is a good guy." Jed hesitated. "Learn anything you can share?"

"No. Didn't learn anything at all. I don't know anything more about what happened today than Katie does, and you know that means the investigation is at a standstill." Adam couldn't share anything more with Jed, but he walked slowly around the house and toward the lane, surveying, as Jed fell in step beside him. The night air cooled his skin as he breathed deeply. "You might be able to help, though. What do you know about Katie's brother, Timothy?"

"Probably nothing more than she told you. He's a stand-up guy and an excellent furniture-maker. Then, a couple of months ago, he stops coming around. He's not caring for his sister's horse anymore, not coming to church services or visiting on the off Sundays. Basically he's nowhere to be seen."

"What about his customers? His business?" Adam looked up and down the road and then turned to walk back up the lane.

"I don't know. I haven't seen him to be able to ask him. I know that's not helpful, but I don't have any further information. It's like he just disappeared."

"But he didn't leave the community? Quit being Amish? Did he and Katie have a falling-out?" The sun dipped behind the tree line, and the first fireflies of the evening began to flash. Darkness was fine when it worked in his favor and hid him, but it could be deadly when it concealed the enemy.

"No. He's still around. There's evidence of that. When I stop by, his dog is obviously cared for. His yard is kept. I've even seen wash on the line. But he's never there." Jed crossed his arms over his chest, a sign of resignation. "He's there but not there."

"So, he knows that you're coming and takes off?"

"It seems so. I've thought of contacting an old buddy of mine in Fort Wayne, but I don't have anything to tell him. There doesn't seem to be any evidence of wrongdoing. He just doesn't come around."

"You're still in contact with people from your…former life?" Adam just couldn't wrap his mind around the idea of leaving law enforcement to be a farmer or to build furniture, or whatever it was that Jed did to earn his living.

"Sure."

"How did you ever decide to—"

"Join the Amish church?" Jed chuckled. "I had amnesia."

"And then you remembered you were Amish?" Adam couldn't keep the sarcastic tone from his voice. But to give up a career in law enforcement, a job that righted wrongs and fought for justice? He couldn't understand that.

"No, but as I worked through the difficulties of my loss of memory, including my run-in with the guys who were after me, I realized I'd been wanting a more relaxed and slower pace to my life. I was ready to settle down, spend time raising a family, eat pie." An easy smile stretched across his face.

It still wasn't anything Adam could understand, although he begrudgingly admitted to himself that he admired the peace Jed seemed to have. He was ready to move on to the next topic. "What about Katie? All she told me was that her brother is her only family left."

"That's probably about all you're going to get as far as information goes. I haven't known her long, but Sarah tells me Katie's husband was killed in an accident at the sawmill. It's been a struggle for her since, but we help as much as we can. And her brother has always been helpful, until just recently. The Amish take care of each other, especially families."

"Would she be helpful in the investigation?"

"The Amish don't like to mix with law enforcement. They keep to themselves as much as they can. Considering what the former sheriff was like, I can't say I blame them all the time." Jed shook his head and smiled. "I should say *we* keep to ourselves as much as possible. It's only been a few months since I joined the church, and it's going to take a while to get used to. With Katie, though, I think she honestly doesn't know anything about her brother. Just give her time. The Amish believe patience is a virtue."

Adam touched his weapon in its holster, his fingers rubbing on the smooth leather, and scanned the perimeter again. For too long he had been investigating a suspected ring of identity-document smugglers. Counterfeit passports and social security cards had been leaching out of the Chicago area and turning up all over the Midwest. Katie's brother had been missing in action for two months, there but not there, and now it seemed that someone was willing to shoot at Katie. Patience may be a virtue, but he didn't have time to wait. The sooner justice could be administered, the better.

Katie might be Amish but that didn't mean she was naive. She noticed things. A lot of things. Facial expressions. Unspoken words. Nearly imperceptible gestures. She had clearly seen Adam's skeptical look in her direction when he had stepped out to take his telephone call. His brown eyes had clouded with uncertainty. The man doubted her, and to some extent she could understand why.

Her own *bruder*, her only *bruder*, was a person of interest. What was that phrase? Guilt by association.

But she wasn't guilty. She was scared and doing her best to trust in the goodness and divine will of *Gott*.

Katie sipped her coffee and forced herself to make conversation, trying not to stare out the window. Eventually Adam returned, and although he didn't exactly smile at her, it seemed that his clouds of doubt had cleared. Perhaps whatever private conversation he had had with Jed had satisfied him.

He grabbed another cookie and bit off half. "Ready to go?"

"Jah." She hugged her twins tightly, cherishing the softness of their cheeks against hers, planting kisses on their foreheads, engraving their cherub faces in her mind's eye.

As she stood, Sarah gathered the twins to the folds of her skirt. Sarah's daughter, Lyddie, stood nearby, just a couple of years older and a *gut* friend to her girls. "It is only for tonight," Sarah reassured her. "Tomorrow you will be together again."

After Adam had checked the front yard, she hobbled back to his SUV and allowed him to help her in. Her leg was feeling better, but she still appreciated his assistance, as well as the cane he had whittled. After Katie waved one last goodbye through the window, the vehicle roared down the road.

With Adam's driving speed, it did not take long to reach home. Of course she had ridden in a vehicle, but Adam seemed to drive much faster than other drivers, with trees and bushes and homes whizzing past at a tremendous pace. As he pulled into her lane, she grasped the door handle to keep herself upright.

When he put the vehicle into Park, she turned to him. His eyes flashed in the dim interior of the vehicle, seeming to reflect the moonlight, and she forced her gaze toward her house and away from him. His handsomeness was not something upon which she should dwell. "*Danki*, Special Agent Troyer. I have much for which to thank you. Saving my life, whittling the cane, driving me home. You have protected me, and I am grateful."

He retrieved a business card from his wallet. "If your brother contacts you or you think of anything that might be helpful, can you get to a telephone and call me? Or if your leg does not heal well and you want to get to the hospital, call me and I'll come for you. Is there a phone nearby?"

Shadows played around his angular features when she glanced at him. "*Jah*, a couple of houses down the road." It would not do for her to find him handsome. There was nothing that could come of it. If she ever did remarry, it would be to an Amish man, not a brooding, weapon-carrying *Englischer*.

He simply nodded and hopped out of the vehicle, jogging around the front to offer her assistance. "I'll get your bicycle and then wait until you get inside and turn on a light."

"*Danki*. Just lean the bicycle against the porch railing." She stole one last glance at his strong profile. "Good night."

"Good night," he called over his shoulder as he parked the bicycle.

She opened the front door, stepped inside and closed the door behind her. By the light of the moon, she stepped toward the propane-powered lamp in the living room, running her hand along the top of the easy chair. If she had come in the back, there would have been a battery-powered lantern at the door. But she hadn't expected to be dropped off in a government agent's vehicle after dark.

On her third step, she paused, the skin on her arms rippling into goose bumps. Was someone else in the room? It didn't feel right somehow, and her heart slammed against her chest. Slowly she turned in a circle, peering into the darkness. The moonlight that had seemed so bright outside suddenly seemed extinguished within the house.

She spied a figure at the back door, and adrenaline spiked through her arteries, her fingers digging into the chair back. But it was only her winter cape hanging on a hook at the back door. Now that warm weather was here for the summer, she ought to store it away.

Her mind was playing tricks on her. That was all. She straightened her apron and inhaled deeply, then took the last few steps to the lamp. With her hand on the knob to regulate the propane, and her other hand reaching for the lighter, a voice hissed at her from the darkness.

"Katie, no."

As if acting independently, her hands jerked back from the lamp and clutched the bodice of her dress. She knew that voice.

A tall figure stepped out from its hiding place, pressed against an armoire near a particularly dark edge of the living room.

She gasped. "Timothy!" Dizziness threatened her, but she gulped air to fight it.

"Shh." He grasped her shoulders and pulled her into a tight hug. A moment later, he pulled away with a quick glance out the back window.

"I have been looking for you. Where have you been? Are you well? Are you in trouble?"

"I cannot stay." He pulled her hand toward him and pressed a folded piece of paper into her palm.

Instinctually she closed her fingers around it. "Whatever you are involved in, turn yourself in before you are caught. I will help you."

"I am innocent. Whatever they tell you, believe that." He paused, the intensity of his gaze drilling into her. "What I do is for you. For the twins."

A car door sounded from outside, and Katie jerked her gaze toward the front window. Adam had been waiting for her to turn on the lamp. But Timothy's hands slid away, and with a few long-legged strides, he was at the back door. As if she were made of stone, Katie couldn't move. Should she run for Adam, tell him she was safe and that she had found Timothy? Or run for her *bruder*, her only family? Then, without a word, Timothy slipped away.

The corner of the folded paper poked into the flesh of her palm, and she unfolded it and scanned it quickly. It was simply a series of numbers. There was something familiar about the groupings of the numbers, but she couldn't quite put her finger on it. Whatever it was, it must be important, considering the clandestine method of conveyance.

There was no time to decipher it now. Adam knocked softly at the door. Her heart still pounding, Katie quickly refolded the note and tucked it up inside her prayer *kapp*. Right or wrong, there wasn't time now to examine her motives for keeping the secret a little longer, until she had opportunity to figure it out.

She opened the door, and Adam stepped in, scanning the living room. "Are you all right? You never turned on the light." Then his eyes seemed to stop at the open back door.

"I am fine." She swallowed hard. "But *mein bruder* was here. He is gone now. Out the back." As she spoke, she spied a figure running through the side yard and into the adjoining cornfield.

"Stay here. Light the lamp. Lock the doors." And Adam was gone, running through the back door and after the figure in the cornfield.

Katie pressed a hand to her chest as if that could slow her heart rate to normal. At least she had seen her *bruder*, and he had appeared to be well. But what was going on?

At the back door, she grasped the knob to close and lock it, when a man appeared in the shadowed doorway. Forcing down her surprise, she opened the door farther. "*Danki* for returning, Timothy. It will be better for you if you come forward."

But as the man stepped through the doorway and out of the shadow, she saw he wasn't Timothy. This man was taller, bigger, with an unkempt beard and a look of malice in his eyes. A scream stuck somewhere in her throat, and she turned to run for the front. That door was still unlocked. It would be her escape.

But as she turned, the man grabbed her from behind, pinning her arms to her sides. "It's not Timothy." His whisper blew sour breath in her ear. "But I know he was here."

Katie squeezed her eyes shut, as if that would block out his horrible threats of how he would harm her if she didn't tell him everything that had just happened. "How did you know we were at the cabin? Did he give you anything? Where did he go?" The man's hands slid into her apron pockets but came out empty. She pictured the folded piece of paper tucked securely in her *kapp* but immediately forced it from her mind. She didn't fight back, but she certainly wasn't obligated to tell him anything.

He pushed her farther into the house, kicking the door shut behind him.

Herr Gott, help me! The pain from the bullet wound seized her leg, and she stumbled. He cursed her, and she longed to cover her ears. But he held her arms tightly.

Over the sound of his raspy breathing, she heard the door open again and tossed up a quick prayer that her attacker hadn't heard it. But as quickly as she could utter the words, he let her go and turned toward the sound. Adam rushed the man, barreling straight at him. Together, they fell into a wooden chair. The sound of splintering wood filled the room, along with the struggle of the two men.

Alarm filled Katie. She grasped one hand in the other in a vain attempt to stop her trembling. What could she do to stop this? To restore order to her simple world? But her mind could barely comprehend the fighting in her home, let alone figure out a way to stop it.

With a punch to the attacker's jaw, Adam subdued the man. Adam jumped up from the floor and drew his weapon, pointing it at the intruder. "Up. On your feet." Adam's voice held an austerity that Katie hadn't heard before. "Now, let's get some answers."

The man slowly stood, his hands on his knees as he

pushed himself upright. As he straightened, he jerked to the side and grabbed a kitchen chair with both hands. In an instant, the chair was airborne and flying toward Katie.

The room seemed to stand still for a split second, the chair suspended in midair as it hurtled toward her. All breathing stopped. Could this really be happening?

Then all was moving again. She lunged to the right to dodge the chair, placing her weight squarely on her injured leg. Overwhelming pain shot through her body. Her leg collapsed underneath her. As she fell, she glimpsed the two men struggling over the gun, her attacker with his hands on the weapon and turning it to point at Adam.

Her head hit the floor as she heard the gun go off. A moment later, darkness swallowed her.

FOUR

Katie! Adam's heart and mind screamed. But as his consciousness absorbed the fact that his opponent's gun had discharged, the only sound he emitted was a grunt as he lunged for his attacker.

The gun had gone off, but was he shot? No zing or ache of injury threatened him. Of course adrenaline would mask it for now, especially as he barreled toward the man in the dark. With a thud, he had the man pinned to the wall. The only thing he would notice now would be a gaping hole in his chest. He would check better later.

The man tried to kick him, but Adam twisted to the side, keeping the man's shoulders pressed against the wall. "Who are you?" He managed to utter the single question through teeth clenched with physical effort.

The man remained completely silent, his eyes burning with fury. His only response was, with apparent great effort, to push Adam's arm back. He brought the gun up to point at Adam's midsection.

No way. Not on my watch. In his peripheral vision, Adam saw Katie begin to move on the floor, a low moan issuing from her. He longed to check on her, see that she would be all right, but if he let her attacker go, it most likely wouldn't end well for either Adam or Katie.

Doubling his efforts with what felt like the last of his strength, Adam brought up his knee to kick the man's gun hand. He missed, and his attacker thrust the weapon into Adam's ribs. Pain pierced his side. *Doesn't this guy ever get tired?*

Adam tried to study the man's features to be able to identify him later, but his vision was clouded with pain and the moonlight wasn't bright enough. With a quick twist, Adam released his grip on the man's shoulders and spun to grab for the gun. But the man moved, and the weapon flew from his hand and skittered across the floor, toward the kitchen table and the remaining chairs.

With a growl, the man dove for the gun as he thrust his hand backward. He made contact with Adam's shoulder. Adam staggered but quickly recovered his balance. He also charged toward the attacker and his weapon, dodging his legs and shoes. If he could get this guy, then Katie's difficulty, her brother's problem and perhaps even the entire investigation could be done and over. Case solved.

But Adam was a few seconds too slow. Instead of stopping the lowlife, he only got the heel of the man's shoe pressed against his cheekbone. The man scooped up his gun but fumbled it, and the weapon slid away. A split second later, he grabbed another chair from the kitchen table and swung it low toward Adam. Adam ducked, only to see him release the chair and let it fly in Katie's direction.

Even as his mind registered that it was merely a

distraction technique, Adam's body sprang toward the chair in an effort to catch or stop it before it hit Katie. The man's aim was high, though, and the chair sailed over Katie's head. An instant later, the chair crashed into the armoire, heralded by the sound of fracturing wood. Splinters from the chair rained down on Katie. The armoire wobbled upon impact, toppling dangerously forward.

Katie lay right in its path.

Adam rushed forward as it began to fall and caught it on his back and shoulders. Pain cut through his upper body, but he held steady. His teeth ground together as he pushed back against the piece of furniture, maneuvering it back to its place against the wall. Katie fluttered her eyes open, a look of terror seizing her as she realized her situation. With pain etched across her face and her jaw set in a grim line, she dragged herself away from the armoire. Once the cabinet stood upright again, Adam ran to the open back door. Their attacker was just disappearing into the cornfield and out of Adam's line of sight.

Adam drew a long, deep breath, forcing his pulse to slow and his nerves to steady with the inhale of oxygen. He closed the door and locked it with both the knob lock and the dead bolt. If the man was running away, he probably wouldn't be back right away. For the very immediate future, at least, he could see to Katie's injury.

It only took a moment to cross the kitchen and the sitting room, dropping to his knees and sliding the last few inches on the wood floor. He grabbed a pillow off the couch and tucked it under her head. Her alertness at the danger of the armoire had been temporary, and she had quickly slid back into unconsciousness.

Now he rubbed her upper arms. "Katie? Wake up. You're all right now."

She tossed her head to the right and then to the left with a moan.

Adam pulled a strand of hair off her cheek, trying not to notice the softness of her skin. "Katie? Come on."

"Mmm?" A raspy cough worked its way out. Her eyes opened again and then immediately widened as she seemed to realize that she was on the floor, with Adam hovering over her. "Is he gone?"

"Yes. For now." He held out his arm.

She pulled herself to a sitting position. "My leg hurts. Again."

"It's bleeding a bit. Can you get to the armchair if I help you?"

"*Jah.* I will try." She lifted herself with the help of his arm, and he gently pulled her into the easy chair. She scooted to lean against the back and breathed a sign of a relief. "*Danki.* Please forgive my complaining about the discomfort."

"What complaining? Your previous injury has been aggravated. You're only human." Fresh blood had appeared on her skirt. "Can we take a look? I think the wound is seeping again."

He looked at the lamp next to the chair. "How do I light this thing?"

She pointed toward a lever on the outside of the lamp. "Turn that lever there. That turns on the propane. There is a lighter in the drawer below. Just light the mantle."

With the lamp lit, she found the tear on her skirt

and pulled it open to reveal the bandage the paramedic had applied. A fresh redness saturated the edge of the gauze. "Perhaps just a new bandage and some aspirin?"

"That would probably do it. Then we'll just keep an eye on it. Do you have a first-aid kit?" He turned toward the kitchen, waiting for her instructions.

"Look in the cupboard under the second sink, the one for washing up near the back door."

"Second sink?" He detoured to the back porch area.

"*Jah.* It is what we call the sink and counter area right close to the back inside porch. It is where we wash hands and faces after working in the garden or the barn, but before coming into the house properly. It is also the place for tending to wounds, but it will be easier if you bring the items to me. Look for a blue tackle box. It is filled with medical supplies."

He quickly found the box in the lower cabinet and brought it back to her, setting it on the chair's side table and opening it for her. He lifted out the top trays to reveal stacks of bandages, ointments, tweezers, rubbing alcohol, cough drops and a thermometer. "You have nearly an entire drugstore in here."

She sighed but smiled at him. "*Nein.* Not quite."

But his teasing had the desired effect. At least momentarily, her mood had lifted and her mind had been elsewhere. Right now she didn't need to focus on the danger that waited outside the house. She only needed to redo the bandaging and feel better.

She twisted to reach the tackle box of medical supplies but quickly sat back in the chair with a grimace. "I cannot sit that box on my lap, not with the discomfort of the injury. Could you find the gauze and the medical tape, please? *Danki*."

With the proper supplies at hand, Katie quickly replaced the bandaging. "The bleeding has stopped. I think it will be fine, in time."

"That's good. No need for an ambulance?"

She grinned, but it was tinged with a touch of discomfort. "*Nein*. Not this time."

As she returned the supplies to their appointed slots, Adam dialed the sheriff and told him of the attack. He said he would dispatch a deputy and be there himself in a few minutes.

Adam put the tackle box back in the cabinet. "I hate to have to ask you to remember him, but did you recognize the man who attacked you?"

"*Nein*, I have never seen him before."

"I've been investigating for several months, and I don't think I'm any closer to the truth than I was when I started, except that I know there is smuggling of identity documents through Northern Indiana and now we have the counterfeit social security card you found. But a good smuggling ring usually takes several people to operate smoothly. And this ring is good."

"*Gott* reveals truth in His timing and when it suits His purposes."

God? She had just been attacked by a violent man, and she was talking of God's purposes? Her calmness in the face of danger floored him. But the memory of his Amish grandparents and their peacefulness struck him, sending goose bumps along his arms. Their steadfast trust in God and the calm that it brought to their lives and their home was something he hadn't fully appreciated as a child. Now, though? Now he could use an extra portion of peace and calm.

Katie's leg throbbed, but she refused to give in to complaining or grumbling. That bad attitude hadn't worked well for the Israelites wandering in the wilderness for forty years, and she was determined to learn from their mistakes. Still, though, a little painkiller would help.

She pushed herself to the edge of the chair, her palms on the armrests, prepared to push herself up. The acetaminophen was in a kitchen cabinet, and as kind as the ICE agent had been, she didn't want to ask him for anything more. But before she could push herself to standing, he was there, holding out his arm to steady her and help lift her up.

"Going somewhere?" He smiled down at her, crinkles around his light brown eyes, the flecks of gold glittering in the lamplight.

But the smile didn't quite reach to his whole face. He was trying to cheer her up, to get her to forget about the danger, to not be scared. Warmth seeped through her at his thoughtfulness, but it was tinged with the chill of fright at who might be lurking outside her door.

"*Jah*, to the kitchen. *Mein* acetaminophen are in a cupboard, and I will make us some tea. Chamomile is soothing, which helps with anxiety. And it is anti-inflammatory, which helps with injuries, as well as aches and pains." And with the tea, she would retrieve her brother's note out of her *kapp* and show it to the special agent.

"Then make us a gallon." He grinned as she reached for his arm.

With his help on one side and the cane on the other, she made it to the kitchen. There she released his arm, and he moved to straighten the kitchen table and remaining chairs. She rummaged around in the end cabinet, moving aside various odds and ends before producing a small bottle. One step to the side brought her to the sink, where she filled a glass with water. As she popped two tablets in her mouth and swallowed, she caught Adam's surprised expression.

"What is it?"

"I have never seen my grandparents take pain pills or even vitamins or any kind of supplement. Granted it's been a while since I've seen them. And they were— are—very conservative, even for being Amish. I just didn't think Amish took any kind of medication."

"Your grandparents are Amish?" That was an interesting bit of information she would tuck away to examine later. A thousand thoughts pinged in her mind, but her throbbing leg overrode them.

"Yes."

Katie put her glass on the counter and reached for the kettle. "*Jah*, some church districts are so conservative that they do not call the doctor. I am grateful that our district is not like that. If *Gott* has been so *gut* as to allow us to discover a way to relieve physical pain, then I am thankful." She held the bottle out for him to peek inside the almost-full container. "I do not take it often, as you can see. But I have it just in case."

She returned the bottle to the cabinet and then filled the kettle. *Jah*, she sought normalcy and comfort in the routine of making chamomile tea, her favorite. But it would take a lot more than tea for her to feel the least bit normal again. Her hands began to shake at the thought of an intruder in her home, a man who attacked both her and Adam, the agent who was spending his evening protecting her.

Gott, help me! Help mein bruder! A tear strayed down her cheek, but she quickly dashed at it with the back of her hand before Adam could see it.

The tea was put on hold, though, with the arrival of the sheriff and a deputy. As Adam stayed with her, the two men searched her yard and the surrounding area. Sheriff Moore examined the living room and kitchen while the deputy took her statement and Adam called his supervising agent.

"I wish we had more information, ma'am, but your attacker didn't leave anything to go on." The sheriff held his hat in his hands. "My deputy is on duty through the night, and I'll have him drive by and walk around the yard several times, to keep an eye on you."

"*Danki*, Sheriff. I appreciate it."

"I'll stay, as well," Adam said, "in my SUV out front and patrol the perimeter every hour or so."

The sheriff put his hand on her arm with the warmth of a father. "Try to get some rest." He turned to Adam on his way out the door, his deputy following. "Call me if you need me."

Adam walked them to the door, locking it behind them. The headlights of the sheriff's vehicle flashed through the window as he turned onto the road.

"Now, why don't you sit down and let me make the

tea? I might need some instructions, but you need to rest."

"Nein." She limped to the propane stove and put the kettle on, ignoring the ache in her leg. The acetaminophen needed to do its work soon or she would be forced to sit down. "I do not want this injury and attack to slow me down or defeat me. *Gott* is good, and He will help me." Without moving her feet, she reached to the cupboard to retrieve two mugs. "See? If I just bend and twist enough, I can get it done."

Ten minutes later, she set two steaming mugs of chamomile tea on the table, along with a tin of sugar cookies. As Adam bit into his cookie, she retrieved the coded note from her prayer *kapp* and unfolded it on the table. She wasn't sure, even now, that she wanted to show him the piece of paper. She certainly had not been comfortable showing the sheriff and his deputy. The Amish separation from the world and the community's distrust of law enforcement had been taught and modeled through all her life. But surely her *bruder* had had a purpose in risking his life to give it to her. What did he want her to do with it? Right now the most she could manage was to trust this man who had saved her life.

His eyes widened as a myriad of emotions played across his face. He quickly finished his bite. "Where did you get that?"

"From *mein bruder.* He did not explain anything. Just pressed it into my hand before he ran out."

Adam leaned over the paper, examining it as he chewed another cookie. "The numbers seem to be grouped into threes. Is it a secret message? A code of some kind? Is he trying to tell you something without being discovered by someone?"

Katie sipped her tea. Perhaps the chamomile would calm the erratic thumping of her heart. After months of no communication with her *bruder*, he reappeared and gave her this. It must have some meaning, and hope in a restored relationship blossomed within her chest before she could tamp it down. "*Jah*, I think so. I hope so."

"It's meaningless, though, until it's deciphered. What is the code?"

"*Ach*, I do not remember. I have been so tossed around today that I cannot think straight. *Mein bruder* was always secretive, always coming up with different ways to communicate so no one else could understand, always reading about spies and their secret codes." After the day she had had, she could puzzle over it all night and probably not have an answer in the morning.

"Of course." He sipped his tea as he continued to examine the paper. "I'll have the agency's cryptographers take a look at it tomorrow. Right now, let me get a digital copy." He retrieved his phone from his pocket and took a picture of the piece of paper, then tapped a few more buttons on the phone. "It's on its way. I'll get the local guys on it as well, first thing in the morning. If it's meaningful, we need to know sooner rather than later."

She nodded and examined the note again. *What are you trying to say, Timothy?* Of course the law enforcement officers were intelligent. But her brother was also pretty bright. If they could decode the secret message, she would be impressed.

"What else can you tell me about Timothy? The more

I know about him, the more information I have to figure this out."

And get me out of harm's way... He didn't say it, but by the way his voice trailed off, she knew that's what he meant.

"All I know is what I saw and what he said more than two months ago. It seemed he had changed some of his business practices, like using a different supplier for some of the hardware for his woodworking business. I saw a company name on a box, a company that the Amish do not usually do business with. One time I stopped by his workshop and saw a different man there with him. Timothy explained that the man was a new hire, but the man was not Amish. He was dressed in Amish clothes, and he had a beard like Amish men that covered his face. But he was wearing a baseball cap, pulled down low over an *Englisch* haircut. I tried to greet him, but he hurried away to the back of the workshop. *Mein bruder* was quick—too quick—to explain that his new hire worked best alone and was a little shy of strangers."

"Did you get his name?" Adam stood to pull back the window shade slightly and peer outside. Seemingly satisfied, he sat again and selected another cookie from the tin.

"*Nein*. Now that I think on it, Timothy was rather hesitant to tell me anything at all. He spoke in that slow way he gets when he is trying to think what to say as he is talking." She sipped her tea, that day and that meeting fresh in her mind. Her brother had seemed odd then, but it had never occurred to her that something was *this* wrong. If she had persisted then in finding the truth, could all of this danger and these attacks and the shooting have been avoided?

"Do you think he was lying?"

That very word, *lying*, made Katie sad, a bit of grief pinging in her midsection, but perhaps he had been. Still, she couldn't tolerate the idea. "We are taught not to lie from the time we are small children. Lying is a sin."

"Perhaps he feels so threatened that he thinks he must lie. He believes he has no other choice."

"*Ach*, I cannot imagine that much danger." With her hands hidden in her lap, though, she wrung them together. Was Timothy's situation that bad? Most likely so, judging by the attacks she had suffered that very afternoon and night. Adam just didn't want to scare her.

She appreciated the carefulness of the agent sitting across the table from her, but she could see the facts, as well. Her brother just didn't come around anymore like he used to. He hadn't attended church services in more than a month. He always had some excuse like illness, which she would see in a note he would leave for her now and then. Was he distancing himself deliberately from their Amish ways? It seemed as if he wanted nothing to do with her, but he was feeding her just enough information to make everything look normal so she wouldn't question him or examine the situation any further.

Sleepiness began to overtake her, and she wrapped her hands around the warm mug. A glance at the clock on the wall revealed the lateness of the hour.

"You need to rest." Apparently Adam had noticed her fatigue, as well.

"*Jah*, and wash and put on clean clothes." A fresh change of garments always made her feel better. It was too bad that she couldn't change her emotions as easily, from fear and trembling to confidence and calm. "What about the intruder? Will he come back?"

"The deputy will drive by, remember, and walk the yard. And I'll be here, in my SUV out front and patrolling the perimeter every hour or so. Will that help you rest?"

The generosity and thoughtfulness of this *Englischer* surprised her. He would give up his sleep so that she could sleep? "*Danki.* And I will try to think some more on the secret code."

"We'll tackle that in the morning, at the sheriff's office."

But as she rinsed the mugs and put them in the sink, she couldn't help but wonder if they would even survive the night.

FIVE

Adam had pulled all-nighters before, but usually with several cups of coffee. Why hadn't he asked Katie to fill a thermos before she had turned in for the night and he had retreated to his SUV? He rubbed his eyes and walked the perimeter of the yard again as the sun rose, stopping to peer through the trees at a scampering noise that turned out to be a chipmunk. Despite his sleepiness, at least they were still safe, thanks in part to the vigilance of the deputy through the night. Perhaps Katie's relief at getting some much-needed rest would override any upset that he had worn a path in her yard.

An hour later, he had had two cups of coffee and a helping of scrapple, a delicious Amish pork breakfast dish that summoned up pleasant childhood memories of his Amish grandparents. Two hours later, he was in the driver's seat of his Tahoe, speeding back toward Jed and Sarah's house so that Katie could check in on her twins. He hadn't been sure it was a good idea to drop in, but the desperation of a mother to hug her children was difficult to reason with.

"*Danki* for returning to Sarah's house. The sheriff's

office is not a place for children, is it? I will ask Sarah to keep Ruth and Rebekah a while longer." Katie's lilting voice filled the SUV as Adam checked all the mirrors.

So far, on this road, he hadn't seen a single vehicle. "Yeah, that would be best. We need to concentrate on deciphering the secret message. And they would be safe with Jed and Sarah." He didn't add that they would be more safe there than with them, but Katie could probably guess the unsaid words.

She nodded and held her breath, as if she were afraid to say something.

He glanced at her profile as she stared out the windshield, biting her lip. If she knew something, he needed to know also. This was no time to be scared to speak. "Something on your mind?"

She exhaled and rotated toward him. "I was so tired last night, and overwhelmed by what all happened, that I was dozing off before I could ask you. With all the physical activity of yesterday—bicycling, running, getting injured—as well as the mental exhaustion of puzzling over *mein bruder*, all the police and then leaving my twins, I was worn out."

"Are you feeling better now?"

"*Jah*, I am. My leg aches a little, but it will heal."

"What did you want to ask?" Or did he not want to know? It sounded personal, and he'd guarded his private life and his background so much in his job as an ICE special agent that he wasn't good at talking about anything except his work. Yet this beautiful Amish woman was so much more sincere and honest about herself than anyone he'd ever met that the prompting came out before he knew what he was saying.

"It is about your last name, Troyer. It has been puzzling me since that moment outside the cabin yesterday, when you introduced yourself. I know there are many who have names that were originally Amish even though the person is not Amish, but you said something about your grandparents. What is the connection?"

Adam glanced in the rearview mirror and scrubbed a hand over his face. She was clearly just curious, but he wished he didn't have to talk about it. His family history was not one he was proud of. Yet one look at Katie and her wide blue eyes, and he knew he would answer anything she asked.

He shifted in his seat and hitched his grip on the steering wheel. That wasn't a good position for a special agent—to be ready to tell all. He hadn't known her long, but something about her wholesomeness and innocence had seeped into him, acting like a truth serum on his hardened outer shell. He liked to do his job and focus on that—seeking justice—not his painful past.

Apparently he had been silent too long, for she broke his contemplation with another question. "Should I not have asked?"

His throat seized, and he cleared it, then grabbed the bottle of water that rested in the console. Perhaps if he shared his past, explained that they did have some common Amish ground, it might help Katie to remember whatever she needed to decipher the coded message from her brother.

"No, no, it's fine." He gulped again from the water bottle and then returned it to the cupholder. "My grandparents were Amish, so I inherited the name through my father."

"*Ach*, I do remember now that you said that last night. Maybe I know them. Do they live nearby?" A smile lit her face.

"No, they're several communities away, closer to the Michigan state line."

"Do you see them often?"

The Tahoe crested a small hill, and Adam slowed to pass a horse and buggy. "My job keeps me too busy." It was a weak excuse, but it was all he could offer at the moment. "I remember just a few visits to my grandparents in all of my childhood years. I think my father took my brother and me to visit because he felt guilty about leaving before his baptism and his complete rejection of the Amish faith. But then, after a visit…" Did he have to finish the sentence and tell her about the despicable behavior of his father? How he had longed, over the years, for more of the love and encouragement of his grandparents.

She placed her hand on his arm, her touch gentle and reassuring. "Why did he leave the church?"

"His running-around time."

"*Rumspringa?* What happened?"

"He got in with the wrong crowd. Started drinking. It took him over. In his addiction, though, he was still functioning. Got married. Had me and my brother. But we were never a real family. We were what the shrinks like to call dysfunctional. Eventually my parents divorced. My mom disappeared. She had had enough, I guess, and I never heard from her again. Then both my dad and my brother were killed in a car accident while my dad was driving drunk." He was unwilling to admit that he had struggled with alcohol, as well. He had overcome it, but the guilt of his poor choices still hung heavily on him. How could God love him, a sinner?

She bit her lip and looked out the window. "I am sorry, Adam. Alcohol is a powerful evil."

Her sympathy warmed him in a way no one else's had. Perhaps it was the sincerity she exuded. Jed and Sarah's house came into view, and he instinctually checked his mirrors to see if anyone was around. All was clear as he pulled into the drive. Before he turned off the SUV, he rotated to her. "My dad wasted his life, but I'm determined not to waste mine. That's why I'm with ICE. I want to do something significant. Something productive and helpful." He turned the key and opened his door. "Are you ready to crack that code and get this case solved?"

A surprised and somewhat sorrowful look crossed her face, but with a visual scan of the property, he hopped out of the Tahoe and hurried to her side, helping her down without making eye contact. Why was he sharing so much of his past? This was just a case. Besides, how would acknowledging his Amish roots improve his life? How could one man working a field, or doing whatever it is Amish men do to earn a living, improve the world? The Amish were hiding from the world, and Adam Troyer did not hide from anyone or anything.

Katie's twins burst from the front door, one of them sporting an adorable milk mustache. They must have arrived in the middle of breakfast. Katie hugged both daughters as one told her mother about the other hogging the bed last night. "*Ach, mein liebchen, Gott*'s Word tells us not to complain." But a large smile stretched across her face, and she hugged her twins closer.

"Go on inside, Katie, and I'll be in in a minute." He withdrew his phone from his pocket. It was time to check in again with his supervisory special agent.

A moment later, the door closed on Katie and the twins as his supervisor answered his call. Adam quickly told him of their safety through the night.

"And you think the Amish woman will be helpful?" His supervisor's voice seemed loud in his ear compared to the quiet of the country morning.

"Definitely. Her only brother is involved, so she's invested."

"Well, keep her safe at all costs, until that message is decoded and she is no longer in danger. We can't let an innocent Amish woman be harmed. That's not the way the agency operates."

"Of course, sir." Adam peered around the yard.

"What about taking her out of the Amish area? Hide her somewhere?"

"I think she's an important part of decoding this message first, sir. And wouldn't she be more conspicuous in her Amish clothing outside the community?"

"Have her change. Buy her some jeans and a sweatshirt."

"It isn't that simple." What he knew of the Amish from his grandparents rose strong in his mind. "A faithful Amish believer would never put on worldly clothes. She has already mentioned trusting God with her safety."

"Okay, fine. She does seem to be an important part

of this case. But do whatever you need to do to keep the two of you safe."

Adam pocketed his phone and headed inside with one last examination of the area. The aroma of freshly brewed coffee assaulted him, and at Sarah's urging, he accepted a second breakfast, consisting of a sticky bun and a mug of coffee, his third cup already that morning.

"Is everything all right with your supervisor?"

He took a sip of his coffee. "I've been tasked with keeping you safe until this can all be resolved. We don't want any more attacks like yesterday. And we have agents examining the card you found, as well as the message from your brother. Those pieces of information could be helpful in ICE's search for the document smugglers." Somehow his words came out more briskly than he had intended. It wouldn't be a burden at all to protect this pretty Amish woman. Adam tried to soften his tone as he added, "If you'll have me." Not that she had much of a choice.

Katie nodded, a somber expression on her face.

As he bit into the bun, Sarah seemed to size him up. "I think Jed's clothes would fit you."

Had he missed something? "Why?"

Sarah stacked a couple of plates and carried them to the sink. "I was remembering the time Jed wore Amish clothes because his were torn, and it helped him not be recognized because he looked Amish."

Katie wiped off one of the twins' mouths with a wet cloth. "*Jah*, that is a *gut* idea. You could disguise yourself by wearing Jed's Amish clothes."

Wear Amish clothes? Wasn't this going backwards? He would look like his grandfather. "What about driving my SUV? Yesterday, at the cabin, I had hidden the Tahoe down the road. It was unlikely anyone saw it. And, obviously, I might be more noticeable if I look like an Amish man but I'm driving an automobile." Were they serious about this?

"You could just remove the hat when you are driving. Then you would look *Englisch* with your *Englisch* haircut and clean-shaven face." Katie tilted her head and looked at him as if she were studying his haircut and facial hair.

Under her gaze, suddenly the idea didn't seem so crazy. "I suppose I could still carry my weapon. I have a holster that fits at the small of my back. And for as long as I'm here, in the Amish clothes, I would be perceived differently by the non-Amish, so that might give me an advantage in a pinch. An *Englisher*, as you call them, wouldn't be as careful with information around an Amish man they think is just going about his business." If dressing Amish would allow him to move around the community incognito, then that could only help to keep Katie safe and catch the smugglers. "It would also help disguise you, wouldn't it? Would you be more noticeable if you were seen with an *Englisher*?"

"*Jah.* Definitely."

Before he changed, he dug the little whittled squirrels out of his pants pocket. As he presented one to each of Katie's twins, their eyes widened with wonder at the tiny wooden creatures. *"Danki,"* they murmured in unison.

It didn't take long to don the Amish clothing, the dark trousers and blue shirt, although the suspenders would take some getting used to. As he buttoned the shirt, he remembered his grandmother explaining that the straight pins a woman used wouldn't be practical for a man's shirt. The twins, Ruth and Rebekah, gawked at him, probably unaccustomed to seeing a man in Amish clothing without the bowl-style haircut. Katie said her goodbyes to her children, looking uncertain about when she might see them again, and soon they were speeding toward the sheriff's offices.

The one-story redbrick building that housed the local law enforcement sat in a remote and quiet corner of Nappanee. For that, Adam was grateful. He would have enough trouble explaining his Amish dress to the sheriff without encountering citizens on the street.

But inside, the Sheriff greeted him with an offer of coffee or tea and expressed approval of his disguise— his blue shirt, broadfall trousers, suspenders and straw broad-brimmed hat. Adam brought him up to date on the prior evening's events, and when he saw the coded message, he picked up his phone to summon a deputy.

A uniformed officer with thick glasses and an even thicker mustache appeared in the doorway before Adam could sip his fourth cup of coffee for that morning.

"This here is Deputy Cravens," Sheriff Moore said. "He's had extensive training in ciphers. Let's see what he can do."

Adam shook his hand and introduced Katie. "Glad to have help."

The deputy opened his laptop, and as it booted up, he examined the note. "As you probably know, Agent Troyer, a cipher, to operate correctly, usually depends on a key. A key could be anything. It's just a piece of supporting information that is needed to unlock the code. But the cipher cannot be decoded without knowledge of that key."

"So we find the key, we break the code." Adam knew all this.

"Right. But there's no telling how detailed the key could be. And without the key, we will not be able to decrypt the cipher."

The deputy peered at the screen of his laptop and pecked at the keys. "I'm going to enter a few of these numbers into my cipher program, and we'll see what happens."

The only noise in the room was the inner whirring of the computer. Katie looked down at her hands in her lap, seemingly uninterested in the deputy's technology.

"Nothing. The program isn't putting together anything that makes sense." The deputy looked at the note again. "Let me try a few other combinations of the numbers."

But even after several more attempts, the computer hadn't solved anything.

Deputy Cravens stood and walked around the room, as if thinking. "What do we know about the person who wrote this message? Sometimes knowledge of the person who wrote the message can help figure out the key, especially if it's something personal."

Katie leaned forward and studied her brother's note again, her eyebrows creasing. "When you use the word *key*, could that be a book?"

"Definitely. A book cipher is actually brilliant because both the person writing the message in code and the person reading it need the same book. And since it's a regular book, neither look suspicious." Deputy Cravens pointed to the numbers on the slip of paper.

"See how these numbers are in groups of three? They could point to a specific word in the book. Then the first would be the page number, the second would be the line number and the third would be that number word in that line."

"And eventually, with all the words, you have the message." Adam watched Katie finger the paper, a myriad of emotions in her expression.

She held her breath as she turned the paper over and ran her finger over a few letters printed on the back side, near the torn edge.

He leaned toward her, the hair on his arms standing at attention with anticipation. "What is it? You're remembering or realizing something." It was a statement, not a question. He could tell that she had figured it out. "You know how to crack the code."

It really was true. It was that simple. Her brother had used their old method of sending secret messages. All those years ago, when they were scratching pencils on paper in the dark of the night, hiding under the covers of their respective beds with a flashlight, so as not to be discovered by *Daed* or *Mamm*, she never imagined their secret code would be used in such a dangerous situation.

She took a deep breath to steady her hands. "*Jah*, it is a book code, as you call it."

"What book?" The deputy had moved to the edge of his seat, but Adam held out a hand to shush him.

With her finger, she pointed to five letters printed on the back side. The rest were missing because the paper was torn. "These are the last five letters of the name of a publisher of the *Ausbund*. That is the hymnal that all Amish use. My brother must have torn this piece of paper out of a copy of the *Ausbund* and used the hymnal as the book key."

"That makes sense." Adam touched her forearm, a gesture that calmed her. Sitting in the sheriff's office with two men in uniforms was not an everyday occurrence for her, and her nerves had been on edge ever since being in the woods the day before.

The sheriff pierced her with his stare. "And you and your brother have communicated like this before?"

"*Jah.* When we were children. A long time ago. It was just for fun."

"But why would a little girl know the name of the publishers of the hymnal?"

Katie shifted under his scrutiny. "I was bored sitting through three hours of sermons every other Sunday. *Mamm* would make dolls out of her handkerchief and do her best to entertain me, but there were still moments of overwhelming boredom. So I read the hymnal from cover to cover. Every single page, over and over."

Sheriff Moore leaned back in his chair, apparently satisfied that she knew which book was the key. "So, what words do all these numbers correspond to?"

She tucked a stray piece of hair back inside her prayer *kapp* as she reminded herself to be respectful of his authority. "I do not know. That was a long time ago." She added in a lower tone, "I do not recall ever knowing exactly what words fell on which page."

"That's a great breakthrough." Adam leaned back as if to relax the others and reduce the tension between the Sheriff and Katie. "Let's run back to your house and get one. We can get this solved and get you safe."

"It is not that simple, unfortunately. Amish households do not typically have hymnals on their shelves, at least not the hymnal we use for service. The hymnals stay with the benches and are delivered to the house that will host church."

Deputy Cravens leaned toward Katie, his forehead wrinkled with confusion. "Benches delivered to a house?"

"*Jah.* We do not have church buildings. We worship in each other's homes or barns. But no one has enough seating for the entire congregation, so there are benches that the bishop keeps. On the Saturday before a church Sunday, he delivers the benches and the hymnals to the home wherever church will be."

"So, you don't have a copy of this *Ausbund* at your house?"

"*Nein.*"

"What about a friend?"

"*Nein.*"

Adam held up a hand. "Okay, Deputy, she doesn't have one." He stared at the floor for a moment, then looked back at Deputy Cravens. "Let's get online. Everything is online, right? Bring up Google and search the text of the *Ausbund.*" He flashed a smile at Katie, but it looked insincere. Nervous, even. "How do you spell it?"

"A-U-S-B-U-N-D."

As the deputy tapped on the computer, Katie picked at a fingernail, eventually forcing herself to stop by placing her hands under her white starched apron. If Adam was nervous, then she didn't have the slightest idea how to handle her emotions. She didn't know much about being online, although she had seen a little from *Englisch* acquaintances at the market and the other patrons at the public library. But why would anything Amish be online? That seemed to fly in the face of what the Amish were really all about.

Adam continued giving instructions as the deputy stared at his screen, scrolling and clicking on his mouse. "If we have to pay for a pdf download, fine. I'll give you my credit card number to charge it." He stood and crossed the room, joining the sheriff to look over the deputy's shoulder.

Several minutes passed in relative silence, broken only by the click of the mouse or a question of *What about that?*

"There's nothing here." The deputy exhaled noisily. "I can keep looking, but I don't know where else to look. There's some history about the Amish. A slew of bloggers and websites with photos and information about how the Amish live. But there is no full text of the *Ausbund* available online."

The sheriff ran a hand through his graying hair. "Seriously?"

Adam just chuckled and returned to his seat. "Well, they are Amish. No technology." He scrubbed a hand over his chin and looked at Katie. "What else can you tell us about the hymnal?"

"It dates back to the 1500s, and it is written in Pennsylvania German."

"German?" The sheriff frowned. "Well, this just keeps getting better and better."

Katie stiffened at his comment but said nothing. She had not written the book. It wasn't her doing. And she had not written the message either. She was trying to help them as best she knew how. "It is our language." It was the only comment she could muster.

Adam looked at her with kindness radiating from his rich brown eyes. At least she had one ally in the room. "That means then, gentlemen, that the book key must be in German. An English translation wouldn't have the same words in the same order for the book code to decipher the message properly. Deputy, try an online-bookseller's site. Perhaps we can get an ebook version or order an original."

A few clicks later, the deputy had more bad news. "I see two versions available, neither for ebook. Both are used. One is temporarily out of stock, with no notice for when it might be available. The other is over one hundred dollars and would take five days to arrive by mail."

"Five days? We can't wait that long. Is there a way to contact the seller and expedite shipping?"

"No."

Katie summoned her courage and cleared her throat, shrinking slightly back into her chair when the three law enforcement officers all turned to look at her. Law enforcement had not always been kind to the Amish, but she was stuck now. There was no way out except to help find a copy of the *Ausbund*. "*Mein bruder* and I had access to the hymnal when we were children because our father was the bishop. But when *mein daed* died, another bishop was appointed. All the hymnals were passed on to him. *Mein bruder* probably thinks I have an old copy at home. The church purchased new hymnals a few years ago, and those would be a different version."

"Why couldn't your brother have just written English words on the piece of paper?" the deputy asked. "It would be so much easier."

"And so much more dangerous for him if he was caught," Adam replied. "So, where do we get a hymnal?"

"We could check the Amish bookstore. That would be faster than ordering through your computer and waiting for the mail."

"Yes, the Amish bookstore." The sheriff was quick to agree with Katie, looking as if he wanted to swipe his hand across his brow in relief. "That would be quick and easy, and we could get this wrapped up."

Adam slid a hand up and down one of his suspenders, then let it slap against his chest, wincing slightly with the impact. "Let's do it. We'll grab a copy of the hymnal from the Amish bookstore and get that cipher cracked today. The sooner, the better. Katie can direct us." He grabbed his straw hat from the desk and put it on. "Thank you, Sheriff. Thanks for your help, Deputy. I'll keep you posted."

But as Katie said her goodbyes and let Adam usher her down the hallway and toward the door, she couldn't help but wonder how Adam would be received in the Amish bookstore. The owners knew every Amish resident within miles of their store. What was that *Englisch* saying? Would he be perceived as a wolf in sheep's clothing?

SIX

Back in the passenger seat of Adam's Tahoe, Katie was gradually getting used to the roar of the automobile. But she prayed to *Gott* she wouldn't ever need to get used to a special agent checking all the mirrors and scrutinizing the surrounding area so constantly as they traveled. And with the speed at which he traveled, she wondered, each time she climbed into the vehicle, whether they would make it to their destination alive.

Gratitude for her simple lifestyle flooded her, and even as Adam checked the rearview mirror again, she observed the teaching of the Psalms and blessed the Lord, trying to keep His praise continually in her mouth.

But did Adam really want to live like that? Constantly checking and being hyper-vigilant of his surroundings? Surely he would be happier, more satisfied, more at peace with himself and his life if he could slow down, relax, and believe in the goodness of his fellow man again.

Katie pushed a hair back into her *kapp*. My goodness, she was becoming philosophical. Did it have anything to do with the handsomeness of the agent and the comfort his presence brought her—comfort she hadn't felt in a really long time? *Ach*, she was better off not thinking such thoughts.

A buggy traveled on the right side as they crested a small hill, and Adam removed his hat and placed it on the console between them. He moved the Tahoe to the other side of the road and slowed, but Katie's palms slicked with anxious perspiration to think of the speed he still maintained. It was an entirely different sensation, and not one she cared for, being in the vehicle that was passing the buggy rather than being in the buggy that was being passed by a vehicle.

"You need to turn at the next left." Katie released her grip on her skirt to gesture to the next road. "Then we will drive past the large market building, and about a mile down the road, you will see the grouping of five shops."

Adam only grunted in response and shifted his hands on the steering wheel. Katie glanced at him in her peripheral vision. His nervousness filled the vehicle, and she felt her legs becoming jittery as they approached the bookstore. She had known the owners, Paul and his wife, Penelope, for nearly her whole life and had many good memories of her *mamm* taking her to the bookstore on a Friday afternoon. While her *mamm* would visit, she had been free to wander the aisles, staring longingly at the candy or running her fingertips across the book bindings, wishing she could take home every single one.

As they passed the market, Adam slowed as a four-door sedan turned into the parking lot. He peered ahead, down the road, then shot a quizzical look at Katie. "Is the bookstore in the middle of a bean field?"

She couldn't contain a nervous giggle, even as Adam scanned the market parking lot for potential threats. "*Jah*, sort of. The bishop from the neighboring church district sold a bit of his land on the outskirts of Nappanee to allow a few of our business owners to build shops. He thought it would help Amish from both communities."

He sped up as they pulled past the market, and from behind the building ominous dark clouds approached from the southwest. "Looks like a storm is coming."

"Mayhap. But it is Indiana, so we may never see rain. The clouds could glower at us and the wind pick up until it drives us off the road, at least if we were in a buggy, but we may never actually see any drops. That has frustrated many a farmer and gardener." She pointed down the road to the right. "There it is."

"Most county roads run parallel and perpendicular to each other so that you can drive in a square around a piece of land. Is that the way it is here?"

"*Jah*. Keep going and turn right at the next opportunity." She paused. "Is this for surveillance?" She snuck another glance, and his jaw was set in a firm line, shadows filling in his stubble that had formed from sleeping in the Tahoe to protect her the night before.

He didn't look at her but continued to scan the bean field and surrounding area. "Yes. I need to make sure of where a person might be able to hide, and it'd be mighty tough for a grown man to hide in those short soybean bushes. There are a couple of trees on the far edge of the field but anyone hiding there would be too far away to accomplish any sort of attack. In my line of work, I always need to be thinking of how to anticipate my opponent's next move."

As they drove the country roads that formed a square around the grouping of Amish shops, Katie could see clearly across the tops of the soybean plants to the stores and the owners' buggies parked out back. "Does this look safe?" It was nearly impossible to imagine any sort of danger in her sleepy little Amish community or a man with a gun in a bookstore, especially an Amish bookstore. But her leg still ached from yesterday's trouble, reminding her that danger was here whether she could imagine it or not.

"As safe as can be expected, I suppose. I'm glad it's removed from the market building and all of that traffic and noise. It's quieter here, and that's the way I prefer it. It's easier to detect a threat."

The tires squealed on the hot asphalt road as Adam guided the Tahoe back onto the main road and toward the shops. With one more glance toward the market, he was apparently satisfied with their current safety. He pulled the SUV into the frontage road that ran the length of the five shops.

The road and each parking lot were bordered by mulched flower beds blooming with the color of yellow marigolds, pink zinnias and purple petunias. An asphalt sidewalk connected the few stores, but otherwise the shopping area really was on the edge of a soybean field. As they drove past, Katie admired the vegetable plants and pots of flowers in the nursery, as well as the bolts of material and sample quilts in the window of the fabric supply store. She quickly powered down the window a couple of inches to inhale the tantalizing aromas emanating from the coffee shop and waved to the wheelwright who was setting a buggy out front of his shop with a For Sale sign.

Adam parked in front of the store and followed Katie closely through the screen door. The dim and relatively cool interior of the bookstore was a welcome respite from the sun and humidity of outside. The owners still ran their business the Amish way, without electricity, so there was no *Englisch* air-conditioning. But without the sun beating down on her head, Katie felt cooler immediately. A few gaslights swung from the ceiling, but they were not lit. They would only add heat to the inside, and there was plenty of light from the carefully placed windows and skylights.

"Does anyone work here?" Adam whispered, his breath close to her ear.

"*Jah*. Paul and Penelope are husband and wife. But it is close to time for the noonday meal. They are probably in the back, making sandwiches." She turned to smile at him and his *Englisch* impatience. But his handsome face was startlingly close, and she quickly stepped away to finger a child's purse that hung on a spinning rack filled with goodies for little girls. Some blank journals with pictures of flowers and birds were displayed nearby, but she didn't have time to shop for trinkets for the twins.

Voices sounded as a door at the back of the shop opened. Adam stepped in front of Katie. She peeked over his shoulder to see Paul, the store owner, emerge, wiping his mouth with a napkin. He stopped short at the sight of Adam and frowned. *"Wilkom?"* It came out as more of a question than a greeting.

His wife Penelope quickly followed, and Katie stepped out from behind Adam, plastering a smile on her face. *"Ach*, Katie, how are you?" The woman's face blossomed with a smile, and she gently pushed her husband forward. "It has been a long time since I have seen you."

The man stopped again and stood near the battery-operated cash register, looking down his nose, through his glasses, which were perched precariously there, at Adam. Paul appeared to eye Adam's haircut, at least what was visible from under his hat, as criticism oozed from Paul like the perspiration dotting his forehead on the warm summer day. Surely Paul could tell Adam was an *Englischer* by his fancy haircut. He pulled on his scraggly beard as he examined Adam. But Adam glowered back, plenty capable of holding his own in the staring contest.

Katie turned her attention to Penelope, who watched her husband with amusement for a moment and then looked at Katie. Her hands spread wide, she asked, "Where are Ruth and Rebekah?"

"They are with Sarah for today."

"Ach, I adore Sarah. She has come through some difficulties and emerged as a stronger woman, *jah*?" She patted Katie's arm. "Well, you understand those difficulties, dear. I cannot believe Sarah found herself an *Englischer*. But then he turned out all right, *jah*?"

There was nothing for Katie to say, so she just nodded her head in agreement. But then Penelope looked away, and Katie followed her line of sight to Adam. She seemed to look him up and down for several seconds and then turned her attention back to Katie with a satisfied smile. "What can I help you with?"

"I need a copy of the *Ausbund*. Do you have any?"

"*Ach*, my, of course we do. That is one book we will always carry, although why more do not buy one for their personal use, I do not understand. Perhaps it is because we have so many hymns memorized already."

As the woman prattled on, Katie caught Adam's eye and nodded for him to come with her. With one last glare at Paul, Adam quickly followed, a strange mixture of frustration and relief clouding his features.

Penelope walked them to the Bible and hymnal area, even though Katie had been coming to the bookstore since she was a little girl and already knew where everything was. They passed stacks of school paper, mason jars of brightly colored pencils and pens, games, flashlights of all sizes, and the always-enticing candy section.

And with each window passed, Adam made sure to step to her side, shielding her from exposure to the glass as he peered out to survey the bean field.

"So, here are the Bibles, in case you need one." Penelope stared at Adam, her gaze taking in his haircut as if he were a heathen, and yet a playful smile curling on her lips. She pointed back to the shelf. "And we have a couple of hymnals, so you can take your pick. Is there anything else I can help you with?"

Adam immediately reached for the closest copy of the *Ausbund* and leafed through it.

"*Nein, danki.*" Katie turned her attention to the book as well, but a small cough from Penelope returned Katie's attention to the store owner. The woman raised her eyebrows at Katie and then looked pointedly at Adam, tilting her head in his direction.

Ach, no. Katie felt heat rise to her cheeks. She didn't need someone acting as matchmaker. Perhaps she was done grieving her husband, but even if she did marry again, it would only be as equally yoked…to a good, upstanding, peace-loving Amish man.

Katie shook her head *nein* so vigorously that the ties to her prayer *kapp* slapped her cheeks.

But Penelope would not leave. "Those twins are growing up fast, are they not?"

Katie nodded as she tried to look over Adam's shoulder at the *Ausbund* selection. "*Jah*, for sure and for certain." She tossed the woman a small smile.

"Are you going to begin teaching the hymns to the little girls? They are a might young, but with only the two children, you probably have the time to begin early."

"We do sing together sometimes as we do our work."

"That is *wunderbar*." Penelope clasped her hands together. "And your friend? Does he help you with the barn chores? Your garden?"

Adam exhaled noisily and cut his eyes at Katie. Frustration danced across his face.

Katie quickly selected a different hymnal from the rack, ignoring Penelope's nosy question. It looked more familiar than the one that Adam was holding, but she couldn't be sure if it was the proper version until she could check it with the encrypted message. Adam looked at the book she was holding in her hands, his eyebrows arched into question marks. She nodded for him to put his book back on the shelf.

"This one will be fine." Katie showed it to the store owner. "*Danki* for your help."

She hurried back to the register, with Adam on her heels. A hand-lettered sign declared CASH ONLY, and she turned to see Adam pulling the necessary bills out of his wallet.

With a final goodbye to the store owners, Paul still frowning at Adam as he stepped outside before Katie so he could survey the sidewalk and parking lot for threats, they escaped back into the Tahoe.

Another sigh erupted from Adam as he settled into the driver's seat. "I was never allowed to utter a single word in there." He locked the doors. "Perhaps that was for the best. That man didn't like me much, did he?"

Perhaps Adam had been uncomfortable in his clothes? He looked just like all the other Amish men she came into contact with, but it must be odd for him to be dressed so differently. "Paul has never been a friendly sort. That could be why he married Penelope. She has enough friendliness for the both of them. But maybe it was your *Englisch* haircut."

He shrugged and didn't answer. Now that they had what they needed, he probably didn't care what the Amish couple thought of him. He had a job to do, and that was all. He wasn't trying to fit in with the Amish community, a realization that struck Katie with a sudden sadness. When Timothy was found and all were safe again, Adam would go on to his next assignment. She gripped the brown paper sack that contained the book. She couldn't—wouldn't—think about that now. Or ever.

Adam started the engine and pulled out of the spot only to pull into an opposite spot that faced the road.

Katie must have had an inquisitive expression, for he explained that he wanted to keep an eye on the traffic going past. He left the Tahoe going with the air-conditioning on high, and Katie suppressed a shiver.

She retrieved the *Ausbund* from the sack as Adam found his photo of the note on his phone. The console in between the two front seats was wide enough to hold the text open as she laid it on the leather.

Adam glanced at the book and then at her. "Considering that it's in German, I think you're going to have to manage this." He smiled sheepishly, a crooked grin slanting across his stubbled jaw.

Ach, he is handsome. Katie quickly stared down at the *Ausbund*, reminding herself that she ought not consider any man who wasn't Amish. Her heart longed for a life's companion, but she knew an *Englischer* could never be *Gott*'s will for her.

She cleared her throat and focused on the image on his phone. "All right, so the first number is the page number. That's forty-two." In her nervousness, she flipped and crumpled pages, taking what seemed like an eternity just to find the proper page. "The second number is the line. Three." She ran her finger down the page. "The third number is the word in that line."

Sliding her finger across the words, she found the word *heart*.

Adam leaned in to look at the word in German. "That means *heart*? I can't imagine a message starting with a word like that, but let's keep going and see what we find."

At Adam's direction, she found a pad of paper and a pen in the glove compartment, and a few minutes later, the entire message was translated. The words didn't make any sense, though.

"I cannot understand it. The words are a jumble." She had let herself be hopeful that this would bring her *bruder* back and all would be well again. But with this nonsensical grouping of words, her heart seemed to stop beating for a moment. Would she fail at helping her only sibling?

Adam stared at the paper in her hand. "I don't see any sort of message there. Are you sure it doesn't mean anything to you? Anything that relates back to the childhood you shared with him? A place or a person, or an activity you did together? Anything?" Desperation tinged his tone.

"Nothing. I am sorry." She looked again at the spine and the information at the front of the book. "I do not think it is the same as the hymnal we had when we were children."

Adam stared out at the bean field. "That's probably why the message doesn't make sense. It's not deciphered correctly because we have the wrong key."

"If it has to be the exact same book, then I am not sure what to do. Our old hymnals were falling apart, and the bishop ordered new ones." A car approached, driving past the grouping of shops slowly. Katie watched it go, scrutinizing the driver. *Ach*, she was beginning to pick up Adam's habits.

Adam exhaled as if he'd been holding his breath through her explanation, a tightness around the edges of his eyes and mouth. The bishop was their community's senior spiritual leader, a man of *Gott*, intent on living life God's way, as he interpreted it, but also a tall, imposing man with a rare smile. Katie clutched her dress over her thumping heart. If the Amish bookstore was not a help, what else could they do? "Perhaps we need to ask the bishop? Maybe he would know where we could find a copy of the old hymnal." But how would the bishop receive Adam, a federal law enforcement office masquerading in Amish clothing?

The bishop? Adam knew full well that the Amish didn't generally like law enforcement, especially in their homes and affairs. Would the man even be willing to answer a few questions?

Adam pulled his cell phone from his pocket, his hand gripping it until his knuckles turned white. "Before we rush right over there and interrupt the man's day, since I'm assuming we can't call the bishop and make an appointment, let me update the sheriff. It's professional courtesy. He's been helpful and has a stake in all of this since it's happening in his county." He cleared his throat to mask the feeling that he was going to choke, thinking about sitting in the bishop's living room, letting the man scrutinize him and see right through him to his evil, sinful past. Somehow the bishop would know that Adam could never measure up to the purity and wholesomeness of the Amish.

That was an agony Adam wasn't sure he could bear, and he'd had to deal with a lot of agony in his life. And yet, was he foolish to hope for that peacefulness that seemed to come with faith? Where could he find it?

"Whatever you think is best." Katie looked out the window as if to give him some privacy for his phone call.

A moment later, the sheriff's deep voice boomed through the phone. "How'd it go?"

"The book doesn't work. We're going to have to—"

"Tell me in person, son. I thought I better stay close to you two, just in case you needed some backup. So I'm at the coffee shop just a couple doors down from where you are. Stop in and we'll talk."

Katie tilted her head as if she could hear the sheriff's invitation, but she remained silent.

"I think we'd better keep going—"

"Son, the Amish make the best coffee and the best sandwiches this side of the Mississippi. Probably the other side, as well. Get on down here and get a cup. You can tell me then." The sheriff hung up before Adam could reply.

If he had had any doubt about what to do next, now there was no choice. They would go see the sheriff. He plastered on a smile for Katie. "Hungry?"

"I suppose, *jah*."

He twisted in his seat to check every direction, but all was well. They had been stationary for long enough, and he was ready to move the vehicle. But the coffee shop was just a couple of doors down. It seemed there was no right answer. With an armed man on the loose, perhaps more than one man, looking for Katie, no place was truly safe.

"The sheriff is at the coffee shop and wants us to stop there to talk to him. He hung up on me, insisting that we have a sandwich."

Adam decided to leave the Tahoe parked where it was, outside the bookstore. If their predator did find them, perhaps Adam would see him first if he thought they were in the bookstore.

Adam turned to Katie with what he hoped was a reassuring look. "Ready?"

"You would know better than I would. Are we ready?" She tried to smile, but it only slanted across her pretty face. Perhaps his look wasn't as comforting as he wanted, but she certainly was perceptive.

"Let's go."

She met him around the back of the Tahoe, and he stepped around her so that she was on the inside, near the stores, and he was on the outside, near the road. He put on his straw hat and then took it off and put it back on, angling it slightly to see if it could have a more comfortable fit.

"Stop fidgeting with your hat. You look fine in your Amish clothing."

"Is my discomfort that obvious?" But his discomfort wasn't really with the clothing. It was with the life he had been leading and its juxtaposition with Katie's simple life.

She simply nodded and looked at the buggies as they passed. He had the sudden urge to take her arm, but this was not a companionable moment. It was a job, an assignment, and soon he would move on to the next assignment and then the next and then the next. It was the nature of his position, a job he enjoyed and from which he derived great satisfaction.

Until now. What was it about Katie and the Amish faith that made him want to shrug off the burdens of the world and be plain? He had enjoyed the little amount of time spent with his Amish grandparents. That was true.

There had been a simplicity and a peacefulness that he hadn't ever found elsewhere. He certainly had looked for it, including at the bottom of a bottle. But when he hadn't found that calm and tranquility there, he had managed to overcome his alcoholism. He did like his electricity, but was that enough to keep him tied to his current life? Perhaps not.

He shook his head to clear away the ridiculous thoughts. With his past problem, he wasn't good enough for God, for Katie or for the Amish people.

As they approached the door of the coffee shop, the tantalizing aromas wafted toward them, and Adam's stomach growled in response. Perhaps a bite to eat was the right thing, something to keep up his strength and help him think clearly. The only way to find the attacker and make Katie and her brother safe was to decode that message. Timothy had risked his life to get that information to Katie, a message that should ultimately keep her safe.

Two steps from the door, tires squealed on the asphalt, a screech that drove his hand to seek his weapon in the holster. His other hand found the small of Katie's back, ready to push her down and cover her with his own body. With another shriek of the tires, he thrust her into the doorway, heading her toward what he hoped was safety as he scoured the street for the speeding vehicle.

SEVEN

Adam nodded a fast thanks as the sheriff pulled Katie inside the coffee shop. He must have heard the squeal of tires, as well.

With his weapon drawn, Adam spun back to the parking lot. He ducked as best he could behind a tall potted plant, praying it would provide adequate concealment. A white cargo van swerved close. A shot hit the cement step below him, sending small chunks of concrete flying. Adam crouched lower, his eyes squinting out of instinct to keep the flying debris out, but preventing him from getting a clear look at the shooter.

The van jerked back toward the road. Adam stepped out from behind the plant, prepared to fire back, but the vehicle sped away too quickly. With dismay, he saw that there was no license plate. With no tag number, the sheriff would probably be unable to identify the van.

Sheriff Moore stepped out from behind him. "Katie's safe, and everyone's staying inside. What happened?"

Adam didn't stop his scan of the area. "Warning shot. I think the driver could see that he wouldn't get Katie, but he wanted to make sure we knew he was here."

"I radioed my deputy. He's on his way."

A few moments later, the law enforcement vehicle arrived, and the deputy began processing the scene.

Adam stepped inside the café, behind the sheriff. At least he knew his senses were alert. Now he needed to make sure they stayed that way.

More coffee would help with that.

He took a deep breath and willed his pulse to stop pounding as he confirmed that Katie was unharmed.

"You're doin' fine, son. Let's sit down and catch a breath. You can fill me in while the deputy searches outside." Sheriff Moore clapped him on the shoulder and led the way to a table near the back. Adam had been an ICE special agent for enough years to develop some maturity in his skills, yet the sheriff's words of encouragement were a balm to his nerves.

Katie smiled demurely and said, *"Danki,"* and then followed the sheriff to his table. Wide-eyed, she nodded to a server she seemed to know, an Amish woman with the same style of white starched prayer *kapp*, as she sat.

Adam selected a chair on the side of the table, from which he could see both the front and the back of the little café. Instinctually he visually scanned and made mental notes of the exits, the customers and what he could see through the kitchen door. "Not many customers now?"

"No, and that's a blessing."

"But now the step out front is damaged."

"Everyone's just glad no person is damaged. We'll get the cement fixed."

The Amish server approached and poured coffee for

Adam and Katie, and then brought chicken-salad sandwiches with a pickle and a side of potato chips.

"So, the hymnal from the bookstore isn't the key to
the cipher?" The sheriff took a large bite of his sandwich and washed it down with a drink of coffee.

"No. We figure it's a more recent printing."

"The copy of the *Ausbund* that *mein bruder* and I
used seemed to be old even then, when we were children. It could have been printed a half of a century ago.
It probably is no longer being printed." Katie added
sugar to her coffee and stirred.

"So, we can't find one online." Adam recapped as
he took a sip of the strong black coffee. The sheriff had
been right. It was the best he had ever tasted. "There's
no time to order one. And the Amish bookstore doesn't
sell one that will break the cipher. I think Katie's brother
must have thought she had one of the old hymnals, otherwise he wouldn't have made cracking his code this
difficult."

Sheriff Moore wiped his mouth with a napkin. "What
about the bishop? Maybe he can help."

The bishop. Adam's pulse spiked. "Okay. Sure."

"Maybe he still has a copy of the old hymnal."

"That's what Katie wondered." Adam's leg began to
jiggle underneath the table, a nervous habit he thought
he had conquered in school. He was a federal agent of
some experience and caliber of skill. Meeting an Amish
bishop shouldn't be intimidating. But it most definitely
was. "I guess it's worth asking. And I'm eager to get
this resolved before someone gets hurt."

"I would be happy to go with you. Perhaps my presence would make the visit seem more like official busi-

ness. Of course there's no guarantee that would help, but most likely it wouldn't hurt."

Katie folded her napkin and laid it on the table. "It is true that the Amish do not usually care for law enforcement. But this is a simple request about a book. I do not think the bishop will take issue with that."

"If it's any help, son, I've met the bishop. I've had a piece of his wife's fabulous strawberry pie, and he seemed to be an upstanding guy."

Somehow Adam couldn't see an Amish bishop taking kindly to being called a term so casual as *guy*. And good pie didn't make for a pleasant visit, necessarily, but since the sheriff had met him and Adam hadn't, Adam would take his word for it. At a loss for an intelligent reply, Adam stayed silent.

"*Danki*, Sheriff Moore," Katie said in the gap of silence, "but we will go. Bishop Zook worked with and studied under my *daed*, and *Daed* always spoke of him fondly. That relationship, to my *daed*, as well as to *mein bruder* and me, will soften him to both the visit and the request. Then *Gott* will handle the rest." She smiled at Adam, dimples deepening that he hadn't noticed before. "All Agent Troyer needs to do is get us there."

And keep her safe, she didn't say. But from the look of peace on her face, perhaps she hadn't even thought it. What would Adam give for that kind of calm about life? That level of trust that the best would work out, that Someone was watching over him?

The realization hit him square in the chest. He would give everything.

Adam gradually became aware of the sheriff and Katie staring at him as he gazed at his half-empty cup of coffee. "Ahem, yes. We'll take care of it. Do you think this Bishop Zook will see me as making an effort, due to my Amish clothing? Or will I be perceived as an imposter?"

Katie gently touched his hand. "It will be fine. *Gott* is *gut*, and He looks after us."

The sheriff made eye contact with Adam, his gaze penetrating to Adam's soul. Then he turned to Katie with a gentler look around his eyes. "Would you like to visit with your friend who's working here? Why don't we see if she can take a break?" He looked to Adam. "I'll take her back to the staff break room and make sure the area is secure."

He returned a moment later and took a sip of his coffee. "Want to tell me what's going on, son? Your shaking leg is about to upset everything on this table. There's something more here than just pursuing a lead in a case."

The sheriff's gaze softened, reminding Adam of the few good times he had had with his father. Adam had been forced to be strong for so long that he wasn't sure what to say or how to respond to genuine interest and concern. To buy himself some time, he took a gulp of his coffee, but he choked on it and sputtered into his napkin. The sheriff clapped him on the back, a knowing look in his eyes.

"I'm just nervous about meeting the bishop. Someone who is harsh and critical of outsiders."

"What makes you think he'll be harsh and critical?"

"My dad always thought so. That's why he left his Amish roots. My grandparents were kind people, but that only caused me more confusion about the Amish and religion in general. I mean, isn't the Amish life one that someone is usually born into? You don't just join them like you join a health club." Why was he saying all of this? Was he that desperate for someone to talk to? He had stuffed his past down for so long and moved into the future as if the past hadn't existed, that now, here in this Amish world, he felt like he was going to explode with questions and confusion.

"Grandparents, huh? I thought Troyer sounded like an Amish name."

"Yeah, but I didn't spend time with anyone other than my grandparents and a neighbor every now and then. Certainly not a bishop." And if the bishop knew of his past? Well, the man wouldn't want to be tainted by close proximity to such a sinner as Adam.

"Obviously I don't know your grandparents, but I think you'll find that most Amish are more like them— kind, generous, thoughtful. They're good people."

"Too good to be around someone like me." Adam toyed with his coffee mug, unable to look the sheriff in the eye.

The table creaked as the sheriff leaned forward. "Well, I don't know about that. The Amish have their share of problems, as well. No one is perfect, not even the Amish."

"Okay, but they still haven't had the problems I've had." And in response to the empathetic look in the sheriff's eye, before he could even think it through, Adam found the rest of the confession tumbling out uncontrolled. "My dad started drinking in his running-around time. Got involved with the wrong crowd. So he was never baptized into the church. He got married.

Had me and my brother. But he never could conquer the drinking, and my mom left him." He grabbed a glass of water and gulped. "Well, isn't there a verse about the sins of the father? It wasn't long after my dad and my brother were killed in a drunk-driving accident that I succumbed, as well. Stupid, wasn't it? I had barely buried them, they were killed because of my dad's drinking and I chose to bury my guilt in the bottle."

Sheriff Moore sat silent, giving him room to talk and breathe.

"I kicked the habit eventually. I've been sober for three years now. But don't you see? I'm not good enough for the Amish. Not good enough even to be around them. Not good enough for God." He swallowed hard at the bitterness that rose in his throat.

"Now, son, it sounds to me like you know a little bit about your Bible. And so you know that God forgives, if we ask Him to. It's that simple." The sheriff scrubbed his hand through his hair. "As far as the bishop goes, remember that this is only for the hymnal. It's no big deal. The bigger issue here is the way you look at Katie and the way Katie looks at you."

A sudden heat smacked Adam in the face. Had it really been that obvious, his admiration of her simple beauty? She didn't wear a bit of makeup and wasn't bedecked in jewels like other women he knew, but she radiated an appealing wholesomeness.

"Is something brewing here?"

Adam scooted his chair back to get some distance from the idea that Katie might be looking at him. "N-no, sir. Not that I know of."

"Okay. Well, there's still time. The important thing

to remember is that what's in the past needs to be left there—in the past. The Amish—and the Lord—are a lot more forgiving than you might think."

Katie peered through the round window in the swinging door, her hand paused before she pushed it open to return to the table. Adam and Sheriff Moore seemed to be in an intense conversation. Whatever their topic was, it had made Adam red in the face. He had a finger crooked into his collar, as if trying to loosen its stranglehold on his neck. Was he really that nervous over meeting Bishop Zook? She could understand that. Considering the circumstances, she would do most of the talking. Perhaps that would calm him.

Her friend, the server, walked up from behind and pushed the door open for her. "Is everything all right, Katie?"

"*Jah. Danki* for the Danish."

"Come back anytime. And I will pray that *Gott* would protect you."

Katie nodded and stepped through the door. She quickly approached and smiled, what felt like a feeble attempt to reassure him. But before she could sit, he glanced at the sheriff and reddened with whatever look the sheriff had on his face. What about her could possibly make him anxious? So far as she understood his job, this was routine. Seeking out bad guys, protecting innocent parties—it was all part of his position with ICE.

Was he worried that if something happened to her, it would not look good for him in his job? Or was he bothered that he was tasked to protect her, because he had other, better, things to do? She glanced at his place at the table. The remains of half of a chicken-salad sandwich sat on his plate. Perhaps the mayonnaise wasn't settling well in his stomach.

"Did you have a good visit?" the sheriff asked as she sat down.

Adam was silent, barely able to look at her. He reminded her of a boy in sixth grade who had sat behind her at school and couldn't even utter her name when she said hello. She had eventually heard through the grapevine that the boy was sweet on her and excruciatingly shy. That couldn't be Adam's problem, could it?

She focused on the sheriff, suddenly unsure what to say or do around Adam. *"Jah, danki."*

Adam stood abruptly. "Ready to visit the bishop?" Without waiting for an answer, he headed for the register, retrieving his wallet as he walked and visually scanning the exterior through the windows.

Katie reached the front as he received his change. His Adam's apple bobbed up and down with what looked like a hard swallow as he put on his straw hat. Then he turned toward the sheriff, who had followed him to the register.

"Thank you, Sheriff." Adam shook Sheriff Moore's hand. "I'll keep in touch."

"No problem, son. Anything you need." The sheriff laid his bill on the counter and reached into his jacket pocket for his money clip, nodding to the server behind the register. "My deputy's cleared the area, but go out the back. I'll go ahead of you and double-check."

A few minutes later, as Adam and Katie waited in the kitchen, Sheriff Moore unlatched the back door and signaled that they could leave.

Adam opened the door, but Katie paused to turn back and wave to her friend. There was no way to know when she might make it back for a quiet cup of coffee with her. *If ever, depending on how this situation with Timothy might turn out.* She immediately stuffed that idea to the back of her mind, refusing to give in to worry and doubt.

She took the door from Adam, allowing him to step out first. He looked to the left and then to the right, toward their vehicle, which the deputy had brought around. When he seemed satisfied, he half turned his head to nod at her and proceeded down the three steps to the parking lot. With one last glance at the cozy café, Katie let the door close behind her and fell into step beside Adam, careful to be between him and the shops, as she had been before.

In Adam's fast SUV, it wouldn't take more than a few minutes to get to the bishop's house. She would use that drive time to pray for Adam and his comfort with the bishop, as well as for a final conclusion to their entire situation.

The cooled air of the coffee shop had been refreshing, but now the heat and humidity of the Indiana summer settled on her with a vengeance. For the sake of safety, they needed to get to the Tahoe quickly, but Katie couldn't seem to force her feet to move much faster than the slugs she found on the hostas in her flower garden.

Adam was a full step ahead as they reached the wheelwright's shop. Her *mamm* had always said she was the peacemaker of the family, trying to make sure everyone was happy and content. Even now she tried to formulate some words of assurance for Adam in his apparent anxiety. Conflict had always been something to be avoided, and now that danger came with it, she was nearly at a loss for what to do or think or feel. At least she had a protector. But now that he seemed to struggle, she couldn't bear it. If she could just find the right words, perhaps all would be well between them again.

Before Katie could articulate the proper sentence, a vehicle skidded through her peripheral vision. She turned to see a van rushing toward her, gunning the engine and coming seemingly from nowhere. She froze. It felt as if her shoes were stuck in the hot asphalt of the parking lot. The cargo van careened over a strip of grass and tore through the flower bed that separated the fenced-in trash receptacles from the rest of the parking lot.

"Katie!" Adam lunged for her as the van veered back onto the pavement.

She screamed, a primal sound from the depths of her being, as Adam shoved her in between two buggies at the back of the wheelwright's.

"Go!"

But she couldn't move. The safety of the shop was a few steps away, but she couldn't turn from Adam. As she stood rooted to the spot, Adam drew his weapon and pointed it at the driver as the van continued to race toward them.

EIGHT

Adam stood rooted in place despite the recoil of his weapon. The discharge was earsplitting, but it didn't distract him from rushing out into the parking lot and firing again into the back of the retreating cargo van.

It only took a moment for the van to disappear into the haze of humidity. All seemed quiet except for the ringing in his ears and the sheriff's boots on the pavement as he ran to Adam's side.

"I heard the tires squealing and the shouting. What happened? Was it the same vehicle?"

"I think so. And he turned before I could shoot, so I only hit the side of the van." Adam turned to check the crowd, but the sheriff must have told everyone to stay inside.

Katie huddled next to a buggy, her arms wrapped around her middle as if trying to make herself as small as possible. A dazed look was etched across her face.

He rushed to her, patting the sides of her arms as if that could reassure him that she was uninjured. "Are you all right? Are you hurt?"

She slowly focused on his face. "I am unhurt. But

may I sit down?" Her legs wobbled, and he grabbed her before she fell, leading her to a bench near the back door of the wheelwright's shop.

After making sure she was settled, he returned to the sheriff to survey the damage. Huge grooves sliced through the grass and mud from the van's tires as it had torn toward him and Katie. Mulch had been thrown all over the wheelwright's back parking lot. Flower petals were scattered everywhere.

The sheriff tipped his head toward Katie. "She need an ambulance?"

"No. The van didn't get close to her. What she needs is for this case to be solved and the danger to end."

"I'll get my full team down here and see what we can do to find the driver. It looks like he left a little more evidence this time. We'll get imprints of the skid marks and the acceleration scuff marks. You said he spun out and changed course when he saw your weapon?" He removed his hat and wiped his sleeve over his brow as he had Adam repeat the dynamic movements of the van. "I'll check whatever imprints we find against the FBI's Footwear and Tire Tread Files database. Maybe we can connect it to the suspect's vehicle."

"That's a long shot, though, isn't it?" Adam pointed to the grooves in the mulch and the tire tracks on the asphalt. "Looks awfully smeared."

"Maybe. Don't know until we try."

Adam crossed his arms over his chest. "Do you know how easy it is to change tires? The driver could just jump the fence of a junkyard or steal them off the rack at a tire shop a couple of counties over. You'd never be able to find him."

"That may be true, but my department is going to do our best to find this guy. I can't have this happening in my sleepy little county. Tourism is growing here, and tourists want to come see the Amish. They should be able to stay in a bed-and-breakfast and buy a quilt or some homemade jam without fear of being run over. I also have a responsibility to the Amish who live here. They should be safe in their buggies as they share the road and not be afraid of being run over by a crazy English driver."

Adam held up his hand. "Of course, Sheriff. I'm just being realistic."

As the sheriff got on his radio to summon his team, Adam walked around the path of the cargo van, careful not to disturb a single blade of grass or a bit of mulch. As he examined the evidence, he glanced at Katie. She seemed to have relaxed a bit, loosening her grip around her middle.

Wasn't there anything more he could do to find her attacker? Sure, he had been pessimistic with the sheriff. In his experience, no suspect had ever been caught by something so simple and easy as a tire imprint. But the sheriff was right. It was worth the effort. Anything that could help end this danger for Katie would be worth it. She had done nothing wrong except care for her brother. And whatever her brother was involved in, she had had no choice in that either. Increasingly Adam didn't think that even Katie's brother had had much choice in the matter. Whatever he had done, it had been against his will.

The Amish were a peaceful group, doing their level best to separate themselves from the world. Adam knew that well enough from the tranquility of his grandparents, as well as the angry comments his father had made on occasion. Timothy had most likely not chosen this clandestine life of illegal activity.

But if that were true—and Adam had no way to know for sure since it was a hunch at this point—then there were two people here who needed rescue—Katie and her brother.

Adam bent to look more closely at the tire tracks on the asphalt, strengthening his resolve to protect Katie and find this suspect. He would do all he could to bring an end to these attacks.

He visually checked on Katie again as she sat on the bench. Her head was bowed, and her lips were moving ever so slightly, probably whispering a prayer. His chest tightened as a new sense of purpose washed over him. He should do a bit of that, as well—praying. If Katie thought it was a good idea to seek the help of an almighty God, then he would join her. It certainly couldn't hurt or make their situation any more desperate.

God, help! Adam fisted his hands. Wasn't he supposed to say more than that? But what else? This was more difficult than he thought it would be.

He inhaled fresh oxygen and began again. *God, I know we haven't spoken for a while. Quite frankly I'm not sure why You'd want to listen to me. But I need Your help. More importantly a devout and faithful Amish woman needs Your help. If not for me, then protect her. Help me to keep her safe and put an end to the danger.* He mumbled an *amen* and returned to his examination of the tire tracks.

An hour later, both Adam and Katie had given their statements when the sheriff approached with a look of fierce determination about him. "There's nothing more you can do here. It'd be more helpful if you got to the bishop's and asked if he still has an old hymnal. The sooner we can figure out that message, the sooner we can catch the suspects, and the sooner I can get my little town safe again. All right?"

"I agree." Adam clenched and unclenched his fists, that same fierce determination washing over him as he glanced at Katie. He needed to get his anxiety under control and do his job to the best of his ability. That meant protecting Katie from being trampled like the delicate flowers that now lay on the ground, flattened by the attack.

The drive to the bishop's house was quiet, save for the hum of the Tahoe's engine and the one time Adam tried to reassure Katie that everything would be fine. But how did he know? Wasn't he offering simple platitudes that were meant to make her feel better and make him feel like he was actually doing something? But had he truly accomplished anything?

He halted that line of thinking as they pulled into the bishop's lane. An older man wearing broadfall trousers, a dark green shirt and a scowl stepped out the front door at the first crunch of their tires on the gravel. He stood on the porch that wrapped around the two-story white structure and waited for them to approach.

"Good afternoon, Bishop Zook." Katie stepped onto the porch and Adam followed, fingering his suspenders. "We have a favor to ask of you."

The door opened, and a gray-haired woman with a plum-colored dress swept out. "*Wilkom.* Good afternoon, Katie. Come on up and sit on the porch for a while. We have heard of the danger from yesterday. How are you?"

Adam inched forward, his mouth open to speak, but with a glance back, Katie held out a hand to stop him. "Actually, Elizabeth, could we sit inside?" Adam suppressed a smile at how quickly the Amish woman had picked up on the appropriate precautions to keep them both safe. Sitting on the porch would leave them exposed to whoever might drive by on the road. Yes, the Tahoe was in the driveway, but inside, there would be a literal wall of protection around them.

The bishop's scowl deepened, but his wife simply said, *"Jah,"* and led them inside. Bishop Zook followed closely behind Adam, so closely that if Adam stopped abruptly, the bishop would surely run into him. Even though Adam was in Amish clothing, it seemed clear to him that the bishop knew Adam was simply masquerading and was actually one of those dreaded law enforcement *Englischers*. But was he still pretending? The Amish clothing was becoming physically comfortable, and he wondered if this was the spiritual life for him. Perhaps his grandparents were right.

Elizabeth gestured to a chair at the kitchen table and busied herself in the kitchen. A few minutes later, there was a slice of peach pie and cup of hot tea in front of Adam. The aroma tantalized him, and his stomach rumbled in response. A window was open just a few feet from the table, and as Adam forked a bite into his mouth, he surveyed the Tahoe, the lane, and the bit of road he could see through the opening.

Katie fingered the handle of her teacup. "Bishop Zook, do you still have a copy of the *Ausbund*, one of the hymnals that were cared for by my father? We need to borrow one, and it would be just for a few days. We will return it quickly."

The older man took a long swallow of his tea before he spoke. "I have a few still, but those hymnals belong to the People. They are under my explicit care, along with the benches used for Preaching Sundays. Why can you not buy one for yourself?"

"We, that is, I did. But it will not serve my purposes. I need one that Timothy and I used when we were children."

"And what are your purposes?" The bishop leaned back in his chair and stroked his long gray beard.

Adam checked out the window again and then leaned back on his chair to peer out a side window as Katie explained the note from Timothy and their need to decode the secret message. He sliced through the pie with his fork for another bite, studying the wood grain on the table before returning his gaze to the window.

"*Ach*, young Timothy. He has been a mystery these past months. And you believe this particular copy of the *Ausbund* will be helpful?"

"*Jah*. Definitely."

The bishop cleared his throat forcefully, and Adam turned to find the older man's penetrating gaze lasered on him. "Young man, is there a reason you cannot focus on the conversation?"

Adam ran a hand through his hair—his short, spiky hair that was most definitely not Amish. "I'm watching through the available windows in case there's trouble. I need to protect Katie from any harm, and if her attacker finds us again, I'd like to get a jump on him."

The bishop continued to stare. "You mean you want to know if he is coming so that you may adequately prepare."

"Exactly." Maybe the bishop understood more than Adam thought he did.

The bishop was silent for a moment while the only sound in the room was the chirp of the sparrows from outside the open windows. "Young man, it must be a difficult and stress-filled life you lead, always on the lookout for danger. Do you have any faith in the Lord, Jesus Christ, in the sovereignty of God, in His guidance and protection? Does anything within you yearn for the simple life? A life that God ordained, of working with your hands and living in community with other like-minded believers, trusting *Gott* with everything?"

Adam shifted in his chair, heat rising within his chest. On the other hand, maybe the bishop didn't understand anything at all.

Katie ran her finger around the rim of her teacup and watched the handsome agent squirm. The bishop was asking Adam everything she herself had wanted to ask him, but she had not thought it her place to be so forward. The bishop, on the other hand, had the courage, as well as the authority, to ask anyone anything.

With one last sip of the tea, she admitted to herself that she had found herself thinking of Adam more and more throughout the day. His bravery. His light brown eyes that seemed to have specks of gold. His broad shoulders that had such strength to protect her.

Ach, but she ought not be unequally yoked. He was not Amish, and she was. The conflict was clear. Would she be willing to leave the Amish faith behind for him? Face the shunning and turn her back on all she had ever known just to be by his side? Drag her twins away from all they were growing up with and all the people they loved? No. She couldn't see that ever happening.

There was an alternative. Could he leave his *Englisch* lifestyle, his automobile, his electricity, his fancy phone, and become Amish? It was highly doubtful. It was, in fact, so preposterous, that she ought not even entertain the notion. And what would he do to earn a living? There was no place in the Amish community for a special agent.

Why was she thinking such thoughts to begin with? There had not been any indication that he was developing feelings for her. Sure, there had been a glance, a touch on the arm, that seemed to be something extra, like a show of affection or caring. But had she been imagining it?

Was she really this lonely?

She shook her head and forced her mind back to the conversation at hand. Adam still had not come up with a suitable answer to please the bishop. Even though he was cute when he was nervous, his cheeks pink from the scrutiny, compassion welled up inside her. "Bishop Zook, the hymnal? I appreciate your fervor for righteousness, but I am also concerned with my brother. If decoding this message will help, I am eager to give it a try."

With one last glare at Adam from under his bushy gray eyebrows, he looked at Katie with a half smile. "I am not sure you ever explained how this particular copy of the *Ausbund* will help you."

Katie blinked several times, but the bishop continued to examine her. "*Ach*, I guess it is confession time. *Mein bruder* and I, when we were children and *Daed* was the bishop, would use the hymnal for a book cipher and write secret messages to each other. I saw Timothy last night, at my house."

The bishop and his wife leaned forward with the news. "You did? How was he?"

"I only saw him briefly, and it was dark. But he gave me a note written in a secret code we used as children. Agent Troyer and I believe that if we can figure out the code, Timothy's message will be helpful in finding both him and my attacker."

"How could this note have meaning or be helpful at all?" The bishop leaned back again, his arms crossed over his chest. "Your secret messages were the play of children. Naughty children taking a sacred hymnal and using it for their own deceitful devices."

Elizabeth placed a hand on her husband's arm. "But if it helps Timothy?"

The bishop hesitated, and then he nodded. "*Jah*, I grieve for the boy, as well. If a hymnal might help bring a wandering one back into the community, then you may borrow one. I will get it."

Katie helped the bishop's wife wash the dishes while the bishop retrieved the hymnal. "You will let us know how this message comes out, *jah*?"

"*Jah*. And keep praying for Timothy."

"Of course."

At the door, Katie hung back as Adam stepped outside first and checked the perimeter of the bishop's property. When he nodded that all was safe, she turned to the bishop. His grip on the *Ausbund* was firm, but he slowly let it go.

"*Danki.* I will be careful with it."

"I know. Please let me know how the situation progresses."

Bishop Zook and his wife walked alongside as Katie hobbled to the Tahoe with the help of her cane. "*Jah.* For sure and for certain."

But as the vehicle door closed behind her, and the bishop and his wife returned to the porch, a bit of doubt wiggled its way down her back. What if this copy of the hymnal didn't help and they couldn't decipher the message?

NINE

"My house would be the quietest place to work on the secret code, and I should change my bandages." Katie waved one more time to the bishop and his wife, and then stared out at the nearby cornfield as Adam backed down the lane and into the road. The corn was just about ready for detasseling—the removal of tassels from every fourth row of corn—but would she live long enough to see the harvest in the fall? How terrible it would be to miss the cooler temperatures, fall foliage and *wunderbar* aroma of pumpkin pie. "May I see my twins again?"

"I'm not sure that's best, but we'll see."

In the short time they had been forced together, apparently Adam had learned enough of the country roads that he didn't need directions back to Katie's. The drive passed quickly in silence, with Katie offering up continued prayer for her safety, for Adam's safety and for her twins.

As the Tahoe turned into her driveway and she surveyed the yard, making a mental note to water her marigolds, goose bumps pricked at her flesh. Something was wrong. She rubbed her arms, a reassuring gesture meant to flatten the bumps, as she scanned the area.

Adam turned off the engine, but when he moved to open his door, she stopped him. "There is something not right, but I cannot tell what it is." Her voice came out only as a whisper.

She continued to scan, feeling like she was looking for what was missing in a child's search-and-find game.

Adam's whisper broke through her concentration. "It's your front door. It's ajar."

Katie's hands flew to her throat, where she could feel her pulse thrumming. "Someone has been in my house?" Visions of the attack from the night before rose up unbidden, and she grasped the door handle to steady herself.

"Whoever it is may still be there." He retrieved his weapon from the holster at the small of his back. "Stay here and lock the doors behind me."

Once he was out of the Tahoe, the clunk of the locks falling into place seemed to ricochet around the quiet vehicle. Katie sat in the passenger seat, her hands bunching and releasing her skirt fabric as she watched Adam creep around the house and peer into the windows. In what seemed like a few heartbeats later, he emerged through the front door. A stricken look stretched across his face. The despair in his eyes forced her from the vehicle, rushing forward toward the front door as fast as she could with the cane to help her.

"What is it?" She couldn't keep her voice low any longer. "What is wrong?" She could imagine all sorts of terrible things happening, but all the people she loved would not have been nearby.

"Your house." His voice was hoarse with some un-identified emotion. He laid his hand on her arm as she came close. "Someone's torn it up."

A gasp erupted. She hobbled to the door, still standing open from Adam's exit. The sight from the door was one of utter destruction, and she felt herself leaning heavily against the doorjamb, perspiration breaking out across her forehead despite the cool of early evening.

Adam stood behind her, his hand on her shoulder, a weight of strength and comfort that gave her a different sort of goose bumps. "Whoever it was is long gone." His breath tickled the back of her neck and the few hairs that she could never get caught up into her bun and prayer *kapp*. "I've cleared the house and the yard. I'm going to call the sheriff. He'll want to send a team over."

Katie could only nod as she sagged in the doorway and listened to Adam talk on the telephone about statements and dusting for fingerprints and setting up a perimeter.

Ach, another statement? How much longer, Gott? How much more? She was sorely tempted to begin a mental list of her woes, beginning with the death of her parents and continuing with the untimely death of her husband in an accident at the sawmill. But she stopped herself before she could go on. Instead she would choose to bless the Lord. At all times. She blinked furiously, but she couldn't stop the tears once they began. Soon they were cascading down her cheeks and dripping onto her dress, despite how much she tried to thumb them away.

And then, as quickly as the tears had started, they dried up. She refused to wallow in self-pity but determined instead to count her blessings. Adam was still talking on the telephone, so she stepped inside.

It took several moments to absorb the depth and breadth of the destruction of her personal belongings, many of them sentimental and irreplaceable. It seemed that every drawer and every door had been opened. Some looked as if they had been ripped off their hinges in a violent fit. The armoire that Adam had heroically saved just the night before was now on the floor, smashed into a dozen pieces. A quilt her *grossmammi* had made that Katie had hung over a chair had been slashed, its fluffy fill falling out. Katie took two steps farther in, peering into the kitchen. Another tear leaked out as she saw that even her canisters of flour and sugar had been dumped. It looked as if the monster—whoever it had been—had stood at the cabinets and pulled everything out, not caring whether or not it smashed on the floor. Several pieces from a set of dishes her husband had given her had been destroyed and scattered over the floor.

More tears sprang to her eyes, but this time they were mixed with something different. It was something a good Amish woman shouldn't feel, and her fists began to shake and her arms began to quiver with the desire to throw something for herself. She was a widowed woman, responsible for two little girls, with no family to help. *Jah*, she had friends, but they were not the same. She forced her fists to unclench and she inhaled slowly as she turned to glance at Adam, who was still on the telephone. Now, to add to that burden, she had no choice but to traipse around the county with the *Englisch* law enforcement officer.

But as she watched him, his eyes met hers. He smiled slightly, just enough to indicate that he knew she was overwhelmed and that he would do whatever he could to help her. *Ach*, so much trouble and danger could *fer-hoodle*, truly confuse, a person. Her shoulders relaxed as she chided herself. What was it the *Englisch* Christians liked to say?

Gott is *gut*. All the time. Even with her house torn up, she knew that *Gott* was with her. It was all in His will, and she had no place to question His goodness.

She bent to pick up a chair and set it to rights, but Adam's strong grasp on her arm stopped her.

"Don't touch anything. We need to leave it all as it is for the crime-scene photographer. The sheriff will dust for fingerprints, as well. There could be evidence here, if we can just find it, that would lead us to whoever did this."

Katie sniffed and swiped away another tear, her heart thumping a rapid beat. "Who, though? Was it the same man as last night?"

"That's my guess. It was probably your attacker from yesterday, looking for something. Remember he seemed to suspect that your brother had given you something, perhaps some kind of communication? He could have been looking for that note or maybe that social security card you found at Timothy's." He ran his hands down her arms. "Whatever it was, I'm glad you weren't here when he returned."

Katie shivered and wrapped her arms around her middle at the memory of the foul man who had pressed himself upon her the night before. But the warmth and comforting pressure of Adam's hands on her arms soothed her.

But as she stood as still as possible, not wanting the moment to end and Adam to draw away, another thought struck her. When this was over, how could she return to so-called normal life without Adam's comforting presence?

Gingerly, afraid he would scare her away, Adam pulled Katie all the way into his arms. Even as he wondered if that was proper law enforcement behavior, he knew he couldn't just leave her standing there by herself. He couldn't watch her cry in the middle of her living room, surrounded by chaos.

She felt good in his arms. Warm and soft. That much was for sure and for certain, as Katie would say.

Slowly her tears subsided. *"Danki,"* she whispered as she tilted her head upward to look at him.

Her beautiful face was so close that he could feel the short puffs of her breath on his face. What if he kissed her? Would that be *verboten*?

His memory of that Pennsylvania German word rocked him backward on his feet. How many times had he heard his father use that word as his excuse for running away from his faith? He had thought that the Amish forbade too many things. And yet here was his son with his arms around a pretty young Amish woman, wondering what a plain life with her would be like.

Sirens sounded in the distance, and Adam immediately dropped his hold on Katie. No matter what was on his mind and in his heart, he had a job to do and he was determined to do it well. Surprise lit her face. Was that a tinge of disappointment he saw, as well?

"Maybe you should wait in the Tahoe." He hated that his voice was husky and vulnerable, but he couldn't seem to control it. After what he had confided in the sheriff, that he had been a drunkard himself just a few short years ago, he knew he didn't deserve a loving wife or family. He might be a failure at his job, but at least it gave him a reason to get out of bed in the morning, a way to assuage the grief from his father's wreck of a life, a chance to make the world a better place so that others could have a better life than he did. And he certainly wasn't good enough to hold such a beautiful Amish woman in his arms.

"*Jah*, that might be best."

"You'll feel better if you're not in the midst of the mess."

He assisted her back to the SUV and helped her into the front seat. The sheriff and his deputy arrived just as she rolled down her window for some fresh air.

"I know I said to keep me updated, but I didn't expect to hear from you this soon." The sheriff slid out of his vehicle and introduced a freelance photographer he said did some crime-scene work for his department as needed. "We had just barely finished up at the coffee shop when I got your call. What's happened here?"

After Adam filled him in, the sheriff turned to Katie. "I'm so sorry this has happened. A home is a sort of a sacred space, isn't it?"

Katie nodded. "*Jah*, and so many sentimental things that can't be replaced."

"We're doing our best, but would you mind going

inside to determine if anything is missing? It sounds as if Special Agent Troyer believes this was related to your brother, and I agree. But we do need to rule out burglary."

She slid out of her seat, leaning on the cane. "Burglary? But I am Amish. What is there to steal?"

Adam offered her his arm, gratified when she accepted. "It's true, Katie, that the Amish don't generally have the typical valuables that burglars look for, things like a cash hoard, jewelry or expensive electronics. But we just want to make sure."

At the door, she continued to lean on Adam's arm as he led her through the rooms. The crime photographer was already busy, working his way through the house and shooting the chaos from every angle imaginable. The deputy followed behind, beginning to dust.

Carefully Adam picked a path through the mess of the house, letting Katie rest on his arm and absorb the surroundings, evaluating what, if anything, was missing. Only a couple of tears leaked out through the process, her strength and courage in this adversity impressing Adam.

As they stood in the kitchen, making footprints in the flour that had been dumped on the floor, Adam donned a pair of disposable latex gloves and opened a cabinet door, as well as the refrigerator and freezer. "Is anything missing?" He looked around the disarray of Katie's belongings, unable to imagine that it wasn't all there in the chaos.

"I don't think so…"

Adam released a breath. "Well, that's a bit of good—"

"Except for a container of cookies I had made two

days ago that were on the countertop and maybe a bottle of water I usually keep in the refrigerator."

"What?" Adam shifted his weight. "Cookies and water? So the thug who broke in and destroyed your house was hungry and didn't take anything except food?"

Katie shrugged. "That is all I see. May I return to the vehicle now?"

Adam watched her fiddle with one of the ties to her prayer *kapp*. It seemed obvious to him that it was a gesture of anxiety. She probably longed for what felt like safety in the Tahoe. "I think so. Just let me check with the sheriff."

Sheriff Moore disengaged from a conversation with his deputy when Adam approached. "I don't need anything more from her. She's free to go. But be careful with her. This is a lot to take in, especially for an Amish widow. Home is of utmost importance to the Amish, and this probably feels like a violation of a sacred space."

"I understand that, Sheriff." Adam promised himself he would be extra gentle with Katie, but then the memory of her in his arms rose up. He shook his head, determined to focus on the task at hand. He should also check in with his supervising agent again and give him an update.

"I'll finish up here, but again I don't expect to find anything helpful. The modus operandi so far seems to indicate a professional—or professionals—who knows enough to wear gloves so as not to leave fingerprints. We have a partial shoe print in a bit of flour, but it's small. Whoever it was was careful."

"That's my impression, as well." Adam held out his arm to Katie to lead her through the debris and to the door. "We'll be in touch."

Back out in the Tahoe, with the key in the ignition and his foot ready to press the accelerator, Adam wasn't sure where else to go but to Sarah and Jed's house. Katie had pleaded with him about her need to see her twins, and her friendship with Sarah would be comforting to her. Truth be told, he wouldn't mind seeing the little girls either, with their twinkling blue eyes and mischievous smiles.

The distance between the two homes had not changed, but with Katie's nearly palpable anxiety over her home being violated and his own constant vigil for further danger, the time it took to reach Sarah and Jed's house seemed to stretch to eternity. Katie's breathing had finally evened out by the time her friend's house came into view, but Adam doubted she would be able to relax or take a deep, cleansing breath until she knew beyond a shadow of a doubt that her girls were safe.

That wasn't going to happen just yet, though. The house was there, but instead of turning into the driveway, Adam drove past at an even speed.

Katie hiccupped as she watched the house, and Adam feared her tears would return. But her voice was steady when she asked, "Are we not going to stop?"

"Not yet." Several yards down the country road, Adam pulled the Tahoe into a dirt road. Truly, at this closer proximity, it looked like more of a path that led to a gate for a cow pasture. "I saw this little drive when we were here earlier, and I thought it might come in handy in the future."

He turned the vehicle around to point out to the road but stayed far enough back that they were protected by thick bushes and trees.

"Are we hiding?"

"Hiding and watching. We don't want to bring trouble on your friends, just in case we're being followed, since we drove straight here from your house."

Adam kept a steady watch up and down the road, even glancing in the rearview mirror from time to time. These few minutes would have the added benefit of allowing Katie to steady her nerves and slow her heart rate back toward something resembling normal.

When he was satisfied that all was quiet, he pulled out of the dirt lane and then into Jed and Sarah's drive.

At the crunch of gravel under their tires in Sarah's driveway, two little faces appeared in the window, noses pressed against the glass. Sarah's face appeared above them, and a moment later Ruth and Rebekah came running from around the back of the house, the ties from their prayer *kapps* flying behind them, and each clutching one of his whittled squirrels. Katie opened her passenger door and slid from the seat to rush to her girls, barely leaning on the cane as she embraced the twins.

Adam stood back, giving the little family room to cherish the time of togetherness. He circled around, surveying the area by instinct. Foreboding gray clouds were beginning to fill the western sky. In a couple more hours, they would be overhead, pressing down their rain and wind.

Katie and the twins disentangled themselves from their embrace and headed toward the house, Katie with an arm around each girl. Adam stood still, letting them get a head start on greeting Sarah and Jed and Lyddie. As much as he had come to enjoy Katie's company—truly he had begun to care for her, although he wasn't sure he was ready to admit that—this would end soon, as all cases did eventually. He would move on in his single life, and she would return to her life filled with her children, as well as hopefully her brother and friends. He straightened some of the gravel, pushing it around with his shoe, as a single large raindrop dropped on his shoulder. With another look at the sky, he hurried inside.

Chamomile tea was poured quickly, but it looked like the plate of cookies had been out for some time. Crumbs were scattered on the table in front of each twin, and there were only two cookies left on the plate. He chewed on a cookie absentmindedly while he stared out the window.

"Adam?" Katie's lilting voice with the Pennsylvania German accent broke through his trance. "Is that okay?"

He rubbed at an eye, bringing himself back to the present. "I'm sorry. What were you saying?"

Sarah cocked her head as she looked at him, a quizzical look on her face. "I was asking if I could organize some of the women to clean up Katie's house."

"Oh, yeah. As soon as the sheriff says it's okay."

Thunder cracked overhead, and the twins startled and then ran to Katie. A few heavy drops plinked on the roof and the window. It looked as if the storm wouldn't wait.

But where could Adam find shelter for Katie? Where could he keep her safe tonight? Her house was a mess.

He didn't want to bring trouble on her friends by staying there with Sarah and Jed. They had, in fact, probably been there too much and too long already. And although his Tahoe was big, it didn't exactly have two bedrooms, let alone a bathroom. Where could they possibly go to find safety and rest?

TEN

Katie picked up the teapot and poured more chamomile.

"It is soothing, *jah*?" Sarah leaned forward and touched Katie's arm, smiling with a warmth that comforted Katie.

"*Jah*, but we cannot linger."

"What? You will stay here. Both of you."

Even as Jed began to shake his head to disagree, Adam spoke up. "There is no doubt that whoever is after Katie knows where she lives. He has demonstrated that he will not give up. She can't stay at her house or even return there until this is resolved."

"Right. So she can stay here." Sarah pushed the plate of cookies toward Adam.

Katie shook her head at her friend. As if Amish cookies could sway the *Englischer*! "*Danki*, Sarah, but—"

Adam leaned forward and pushed the cookie plate back toward Katie. "But she—"

Impulsively Katie waved her hand in Adam's direction, and he stopped talking. She surprised herself with her boldness in interrupting him, but perhaps enough danger on the run had strengthened her. "I cannot accept. I will not bring danger onto your house."

Sarah paused as she examined Katie. Finally she sighed. "If that is what you think is best. But where will you go?"

"I do not know. I would not want to bring trouble onto any of the People."

"*Ach*, why did I not think of it before? You can stay at *mein bruder*'s. He will be moving here from Lancaster County soon and has purchased a house. There are a few furnishings that I had extra and loaned to him until his things are moved. It is just a table and chairs, a few plates, glasses. But he is gone for another couple of weeks because he has business to finish up there before he can move here."

"Are you sure?"

"*Jah*, for sure and for certain. I am cleaning and fixing it up for him in the interim, so right now it is empty."

Adam stood as if signaling that it was time to go. "How far is it?"

"It is only a couple of miles away." Sarah looked at Katie. "It is the old Hochstetler place."

Katie nodded and hugged her twins again as Sarah rose to gather some drinks and snacks for them. She had known the Hoschtetlers and knew the house to be a fine, old structure. It would be plenty adequate for their needs. Adam headed toward the door, and Katie knew it was time to leave. Her heart twisted within the confines of her chest, aching fiercely at her current separation from her daughters. But what could she do? There was not anything at all that she could think of except to continue to run and hide with the *Englischer* until the danger passed, since she would never be willing to stray very far from her Amish community. Keeping her distance was the safest for her and for her daughters.

She pulled her twins close and whispered, "*Mein liebchen.* My darlings." She kissed each cheek in turn. "I will be back as soon as I can."

The stop at Jed and Sarah's had been all too short, but it had been a comfort and a relief to hold her children again, even if just for a moment. Their sweetness and innocence had dispelled some of the depression that seemed to linger about her. An impression struck her that that could have been the last time she would see them. It would certainly be safer for them if she stayed away lest she lead her attacker to her children.

Katie easily directed Adam to the Hochstetler place. She stayed in the Tahoe while he checked out the property, both outside and in. Seemingly satisfied with its distance from nearby Amish houses, he retrieved a flashlight from the glove compartment and ushered her inside. At his direction, she stood just inside the door while he found sleeping bags and a battery-operated lantern in the back of his Tahoe.

The furnishings were definitely sparse, with the table and four chairs that Sarah had mentioned as the only furniture on the expansive first floor. Even if she didn't have a leg wound that would ache from climbing the stairs, there was no point in checking the upper level. Those rooms were sure to be barren, as well. It didn't matter. She hoped not to be in the house long.

Night had fallen as they had driven, so Adam flipped the switch to the lantern and led the way to the kitchen table, motioning Katie to a chair. He took the chair opposite, setting the bishop's copy of the *Ausbund* between them. "You still have the note?" He glanced at her prayer *kapp*. "Or should I pull it up on my phone?"

She reached up to her head covering and retrieved the paper. "I have it." She unfolded it, placed it on the surface between them and then opened the hymnal. After checking the numbers her brother had written in the message, she turned to the appropriate page in the book.

Adam turned sideways in his chair, craning his neck to see both the hymnal and the paper. "This isn't working." He stood and circled the table, sitting in the chair to her left.

She continued searching for the proper page, line and word according to the message her *bruder* had written in the book code. Adam's scent of the woods in springtime tickled her senses, and she doubled her efforts at concentrating on the code.

As she worked on the fifth word of the message, her right hand, holding the pencil, brushed against Adam's hand as it rested on the table between them. A tremor raced up her arm at his touch, but she forced herself to hold the writing utensil steady. She glanced at him to see if he had noticed her reaction and was struck by the handsomeness of his angular face in the lamplight. *Ach, I ought not to be having those thoughts!*

"What does all this mean?" His voice sounded husky to her ears, but he was probably just trying to keep his voice low and not break her concentration.

"It is High German, the language of the *Ausbund*. I will translate it after I get the complete message."

She continued on, intent on the book in the low lamplight, trying not to worry about her own safety or the safety of her girls. She carefully wrote out each German word above its corresponding numbers on her brother's note. "There it all is. Now for the English."

A few minutes later, she read it aloud, pointing to each German word as Adam followed along. "Help me. Harm soon. Deliver identity. In shadow of old saw place near tree. Come mid night. Three day."

Intensity creased the lines on Adam's forehead. "So, he needs help to avoid further harm. And it's urgent."

"*Jah*, seems so." Despite the heat and humidity in the house, a chill crept up Katie's arms.

"He's delivering something, or something is being delivered. Perhaps more identification documents, more like that counterfeit social security card you found in his workshop. What could *old saw place* mean?"

The chill seized Katie's shoulders and threatened to wind itself around her neck. She didn't want to think it, but could it be possible? Did her brother mean the sawmill, the location of her husband's horrible and untimely death?

Dizziness threatened as she remembered that day she had been summoned to the terrible scene. The sawmill was a place she had not been back to and had in fact avoided with a passion since then. She must have begun trembling, for Adam put his arm around her as if to stop her shivering. "What is it? What's the matter?"

She swallowed hard, though it did nothing to dispel the lump that had formed in her esophagus. "I think he means the sawmill."

"Oh. Did something bad happen there?"

But the look on her face must have answered his question.

* * *

Adam felt himself being torn in two. Was this why most special agents weren't married? A beautiful woman needed comforting. His comforting. And he wanted to provide it, to hold Katie in his arms again.

But he also needed to act on this message, now that he knew what it meant. Something big was going to go down. He knew where and he knew when. He needed to contact his supervising special agent and get the team mobilized. Katie's brother had taken a huge risk in his desperation to seek help, probably hoping that she could contact law enforcement despite the Amish reluctance to involve *Englishers*.

Which was his priority?

Even with his arm still around Katie, he pulled his phone close to make the call. Of course his priority was to catch the bad guys. Justice must be done. That was why he was a special agent. That was his reason for waking up every morning, for getting out of bed, for putting one foot in front of the other. And as long as the bad guys were on the loose, wreaking their havoc, the woman he wanted to comfort was in danger.

Then again, if he could put an end to this chase, perhaps there could be more time spent with the lovely Amish woman.

What? He shook his head and pulled his arm from around Katie, focusing on his phone. There could not be more time spent with the Amish woman, for one simple reason. She was Amish. He was not. That would be the end of their love story.

He tapped the button to speed-dial his supervisor and relayed the new information. It was all starting to come together, although Adam still wanted to in-terrogate Katie's brother to get the details. With this heads-up as to when and where the big transaction was taking place, Adam and his supervisor determined that an ICE team should be at the sawmill at midnight the next night. Factoring in the time that had lapsed since Timothy had snuck his note to Katie, it seemed that the night for the meet-up was tomorrow. As he spoke to his supervisor, Katie sat beside him, her eyes closed and her lips moving in what Adam guessed was a silent prayer that they could rescue her brother from whatever he had been forced into.

As he finished the call, Katie opened her eyes and focused on him. "How do you think Timothy became mixed up in this?"

"I'm not sure, but I plan to ask him when I get a chance." Adam's blood pounded through his arteries as he thought of all the trouble Timothy had put on his sister. "He must be seeking help to stop these crim-inals and protect both himself and you. Without his note, we wouldn't have any idea where to find him or these thugs."

"I have wondered what you must think of my brother, Adam. But I believe he must be in agony over what he has been forced to do. I do not think he chose that life of secrecy and, perhaps, crime." She pleaded with him for a moment with her wide, dark blue eyes, then looked down at the table, her delicate lashes hid-ing the flashing of her eyes.

"Probably. And perhaps when that man came after you, Timothy knew his usefulness to them was done and it would only be a matter of time before he and you would be eliminated." At that horrible thought, his arm moved without his permission to rest on the back of Katie's chair.

"Eliminated? *Ach*, that is what this is all about." A tear escaped, but she waved a hand at Adam to ward him off. "Of course I knew that already. I am Amish, but I am not ignorant of the ways of evil. It just can be hard to admit."

"To the best of my ability, I will make sure that all is all right. You're safe now, and I'll do whatever is necessary to protect you." He fought hard not to gather her in his arms. This was business, and he was determined to remain professional.

"Even at the sawmill?"

Adam cut his eyes at Katie even as his mind spun, trying to figure out why she would ask about that particular location. "Why would you think you're going to the sawmill?" With the probable danger there, in the midst of that transaction, whatever it was, there was no way he would allow her to go to the sawmill. He would tuck her away someplace safe to wait out the meeting.

"Because I am. My brother will most likely be there. I need to encourage and support him, no matter how difficult it is to return there."

Apparently there was more here he needed to know. "Why difficult? And when have you been there before?"

"That is where my husband was killed."

Adam gasped, experiencing a feeling in his chest as if he'd been hit by a truck. Her bravery, her willingness to return to a place that must hold untold trauma, all in service to her brother, astounded him. "What happened?"

She swallowed and then began. "My husband used

to work part-time there while we were trying to get our farm going. I was selling baked goods to help pay the bills, but I had twin toddlers underfoot and could not do much. I was also pregnant with our third child and having a rough time of it."

"Third child?" Adam shook his head. Katie only had the two girls. He hated to think what had happened to that baby.

"*Jah.* And then my neighbor came running into the kitchen one day. She said there had been an accident, and I needed to get to the sawmill right away. She had summoned the Amish Taxi, and it was waiting to take me there." She ran her hand across the smooth wood of the table. "They did not know I had arrived, and I saw everything. I saw…him. His mangled body."

A look of horror swept over her face, and she dissolved into tears. Adam put his hand over hers, the softness of her skin contrasting with the rough wood of the tabletop, and whispered a prayer for comfort.

"The trauma was too much, and I miscarried." She sniffed and swiped away some tears. "It was a boy."

"Are you sure you want to go back?"

"*Jah*, I must go back. For Timothy. He is my only family. I am afraid of the memories at the sawmill, and I am afraid of the bad men. But I am more afraid of losing Timothy forever. If there is something I can do, then I will do it."

Adam was not convinced that Katie should be at the sawmill at the appointed time, especially not since the place was surrounded by such great emotional difficulty. If it came right down to it, his duties did not include her emotional well-being. At least according to

ICE regulations. Would her presence be a distraction to him? But there was no point in concerning himself with it now. He would know more as the time approached.

"I admire and applaud your tenacity. But we're in this together, remember? I'm doing everything I can to resolve your and your brother's difficulties." He didn't want to see her hurt. But did his increasing emotional attachment to her impair his judgment? Absentmindedly he rubbed his thumb over the back of her silky hand.

She shivered and looked up at him, fear in her eyes, her lower lip trembling. The lantern cast a soft glow over the room, throwing shadows into the corners and around the edges. How easy it would be to kiss her.

But it would be wrong. Very wrong. His mind shouted at him to leave her alone. Nothing could come of an Amish-*Englisch* romance. Absolutely nothing.

How could he change the way his heart was feeling about her? He couldn't stop it. It was involuntary. Perhaps it was simply a reaction to the close quarters and being on the run. But what if it wasn't? He had never been in love before, never allowed himself to be that vulnerable and never been willing to admit that he was a person who wanted to be loved. Is that what this was—the beginning of love? What if he did want a love and a family to call his own? Was that wrong?

He leaned down, his lips an inch from hers. Her breath came in short puffs. Was that anticipation?

For the briefest of moments, he gently touched his lips to hers. Electricity seemed to crackle around them.

A huge crack of thunder pounded on the roof and sent shudders through the walls of the house. Lightning turned night into day. In that moment, Adam saw, in an instant, a flash of regret across her beautiful face as brilliant and clear as the lightning.

Yes, it was wrong to want a family of his own. He had a commitment to justice. But not only that—he would never be deserving of Katie. Not even close.

She shoved the chair back and stood in a rush, crossing quickly to the window, hugging her arms around her middle. Another flash of lightning made a jagged streak across the sky, lighting up the yard. But her gasp and exclamation drove all agonizingly romantic thoughts from his head.

"I think someone is out there!"

ELEVEN

The thunder was delayed by only a second, and it clapped overhead. The windows rattled in their casements, seeming to shake some sense into her head. What had she been thinking? She had been *ferhoodled* by the handsome face and strong shoulders and protective attitude of this *Englischer*, for sure and for certain. Admiration was one thing. But a kiss? That seemed too much like commitment.

But it wasn't only the *Englischer* watching out for her. *Gott* was watching out for her, protecting her from the *Englischer*. The summer thunderstorm had arrived in just the right timing to bring her back to her Amish reality. She shook her head as if to clear the cobwebs formed by her attraction to Adam, and if he took it as a *nein*, then all the better.

She turned back toward the window. The severe storm had rolled in fast. Lightning had lit up the outside like daytime, but for that split second, it was enough. She stared out into the dark. Had she really seen someone, or had it just been her imagination, fueled by fear?

Then lightning struck again, this time cracking a tree

wide-open, half of it toppling to the side. As it fell, a person ran to the left, seeming to hide behind another tree or the nearby shed.

She spun away from the window and pressed herself against the wall, her heart beating a wild tempo. "Adam," she cried out. "There is someone there."

He slid the button on the battery-powered lantern and plunged the house into darkness. Quickly and quietly, he crossed to the window, hiding himself against the wall on the opposite side from Katie. He held a finger to his lips to signal that she should remain silent, and Katie closed her eyes in an attempt to calm her rapid breathing.

But when lightning struck again, she opened them quickly, unwilling to miss anything. She wanted to see everything that she could in case it would be helpful to Adam. And in that flash of light, she saw a figure run from behind the shed to a tree closer to the house. He held something in his hand, but it didn't look like a gun.

Adam stayed steady but narrowed his eyes at the man. "Is that his tactic?" His voice was so low that Katie thought he must be talking to himself. "That's pretty extreme."

And then, in the space of a heartbeat, as Adam moved away from the window in reaction to the man outside, pulling Katie with him, a light sparked and flared up in the darkness outside.

"Let's move!" He grabbed Katie's shoulders and spun her to face away from the door that was right next to the window. Adam pushed her down and away from the door but stayed right behind her. He was too slow, though.

The door exploded in a flash of light and flame. Adam served as a human shield, protecting her from the blast. The door flung into him, pushing him against her and hurling both of them against the far wall. She cried out in pain as her foot caught on a chair, pulling on her leg and ripping her gunshot wound open.

Katie clutched at the injury as Adam pushed the door off them and then drew his weapon from the holster. She curled onto her side to see him crawl to the door and fire his weapon into the night. Large, hot flames licked at the doorjamb and the base of the kitchen cabinets. In the glow of the fire, she saw the man run away through the pasture and toward the woods. Lightning sizzled again as if to help her see his escape.

Adam watched through the door a minute more and then turned back to help her sit up. "He's gone, but that's no guarantee he won't be back."

"What was that? A bomb?"

"Kind of. It was a homemade incendiary device." He grabbed a couple of dish towels from the countertop and handed them to her. She immediately applied direct pressure to her oozing wound. "Most likely a Molotov cocktail."

"Something that explodes."

"Yeah."

The door was completely on fire, as well as the edge of the floor and the kitchen cabinet closest to the door. The odor of gasoline and the acrid smell of fire filled her nostrils. Flames licked up the walls, higher and higher, as she pressed the towels to her leg. The heat threatened to burn her skin and singe her hair.

Adam's jaw was set with grim determination as he

surveyed the increasing flames. "Fire extinguisher?" Even as he asked, he ran to the kitchen to begin flinging open cabinets. "Under the sink?"

"If there is one—"

But Adam pulled open what looked like it should have been used as a broom closet and then held up a fire extinguisher triumphantly. He blew dust off the top and the handle. "Pray it works."

Katie maneuvered herself to a standing position, despite the deep throbbing in her leg. She pulled the towels away and began beating at the flames with them, but Adam motioned for her to sit. "You stay put. Don't injure yourself further. This extinguisher will do it."

With a little extra tugging, the pin came loose. Adam swept the nozzle of the extinguisher's hose across the base of the flames, slowly dousing them. As the foam squirted onto the fire, he stayed low and as much away from the door as he could manage.

After several minutes with the extinguisher, the fire was finally out. Katie drew a deep, ragged breath, ignoring as best she could the overpowering odor of smoke that burned her nostrils, and tried to put on a brave face for the pain. But the truth was that it hurt something fierce and it still trickled blood. It must have shown in her face, for Adam retrieved his phone from the table and slid to her side on the wood floor. He tapped three numbers and then spoke for a few seconds, giving their location.

"I called nine-one-one, but I don't think we should wait for an ambulance or backup law enforcement. They could take too long to get here. You need the emergency room now. I can call the sheriff personally on the way. Plus it'll be safe there."

She simply nodded, relief flooding her when Adam lifted her into his arms and carried her to the Tahoe. He settled her into the front seat and then jogged around to the driver's side. Soon they were speeding down the country road, toward the closest hospital.

"I'm afraid our presence there caused great damage to the house." His voice was apologetic.

"*Jah*, and I am sorry, as well. We Amish take care of each other, though."

"Perhaps if we had found somewhere else. Somewhere far away?"

"*Nein*. We are a community. They would not have wanted me to leave, even for safety." The thought of leaving sent a tremor of fear through her. Then, with her eyes closed, she let the darkness flow over her.

The glow of the GPS monitor set in the dashboard drew Adam to check that he was headed in the right direction. So far he was fine, but it looked like it might get a little tricky when they got to the city. He pulled his cell phone out and quickly called the sheriff, who said he would get to the Hochstetler place immediately.

Katie's labored breathing also drew his attention, but so far she seemed to be handling it with strength, as she kept a firm hand on the wound. The dish towels were soaked with her blood, but the bleeding did seem to be slowing now that she was sitting still. The inside of the Tahoe smelled like a fireplace, but at least they were alive.

"How long until we are at the hospital?"

He glanced at the GPS screen again. "Should be about twenty minutes. Are you all right until we get there?"

"*Jah.* It does not hurt that much." But as she shifted in her seat, a grimace told Adam otherwise.

"Can you tell me more about this…this bomb? What did you call it?"

"A Molotov cocktail. It's a…yeah, a homemade bomb." Giving it a fancy name didn't take away the damage it had caused.

"How does it work?"

"It's simply a flammable substance like gasoline, perhaps with some motor oil mixed in, in a breakable glass bottle. Then it just needs a wick to ignite it, like a bit of cloth or a rag, often soaked in alcohol. Could be kerosene, as well."

"I have all those things at home."

"I'm sure you do. Lots of folks do. That's probably why he used that method. He may even have found all of that in the storage shed out back."

"It is worrisome that there are the makings of a bomb around most houses."

"Well, but you aren't going to be making any bombs." Following the blue dot on the GPS screen, Adam turned onto another country road.

"That is true. So, this man would just light the wick, like lighting a candle or a kerosene lamp?"

"Yeah. Light it up and throw it at the target. The bottle smashes when it hits. So then the flame from the wick ignites the fuel that was inside the glass bottle. Boom! There's a fireball that spreads flames. The attacker thinks his mission is accomplished."

"*Ach*, what a terrible thing to do to someone. Why would someone want to do such evil?"

"That's what we're trying to find out." But as they fell silent, Adam couldn't help but wonder at her innocence. She clearly had lived a protected life. Some might even say it was sheltered. Was that best, or did she need to know more of the real world?

He stopped at a light and turned to admire her in the red glow. What was wrong with sheltering, anyway? He thought of the guys he knew in ICE. Many of those agents ate antacids like candy or took blood-pressure medication even though they were still young. They might say they were fulfilled in their jobs, but were they truly satisfied? Pleased with their situations and relaxed about the future? Perhaps he would be happier or more content if he lived a sheltered life like it seemed Katie did. Sometimes the things he knew about the evil in the world and what he had experienced on the job felt downright oppressive and overwhelming.

The light turned green, and he pressed on the accelerator. He could hear her whispering again. With a sideways glance, he saw that her lips were moving in what must be silent prayer. He could probably stand to do a little more praying himself. She had certainly been a good influence on him in such a short time, coming along at just the right moment. Just as he was beginning to feel like a crusty curmudgeon, too far from God.

How much did this relationship mean to him? It had only been a short time that they had known each other, and yet she had influenced him in ways he never would have imagined. Even if nothing came of it and they never spoke again, he would always be changed because of their time together.

Adam scoured a hand through his hair. Was he going soft? *Stop thinking about the girl and think about the job.*

A couple of turns later, the lights of the hospital loomed ahead.

The emergency room was quiet, and a nurse wheeled a chair out for Katie. Inside, Katie gave her basic information, explained the nature of her wound and then was wheeled back to an examination room. Adam followed, but as soon as the nurse was ready to examine the wound, she turned to him and said, "Perhaps you'd like to wait outside. Unless you're the patient's husband?"

Katie giggled as Adam choked a cough into his arm. "*Nein.* He is not my husband."

Despite Adam's discomfort with the question, he was glad for a lighthearted moment for her. Perhaps it would provide some relief from the intensity of the chase. "I'll…I'll just wait out there. Could you let me know when you're done?"

"Of course."

He stepped toward the exit and then turned back. "It's not life-threatening, is it?" He must sound like a moron. She hadn't been brought in on a stretcher or unconscious or any other number of ways a person could be brought into the ER when life was ebbing away.

The nurse smiled at him, a teasing look in her eye. "I haven't seen much of the wound yet, but from what you and the young lady said, I'm guessing she just needs the stitching repaired and maybe some antibiotics to prevent infection."

"Okay. Sure. I'll let you get to work." An overwhelming urge to comfort Katie with a kiss on the forehead swept over him. But he denied it, pressing it back deep down inside, where it belonged. It wouldn't be professional, and it wouldn't be appropriate in front of the nurse.

Adam left the bay, with his hat in his hands, and the nurse jerked the curtain shut behind him. The curtain rings screeched on the rod above, and the breeze from the curtain ruffled his shirtsleeves. He meandered to the empty waiting room, uncertain what to do with himself now that it seemed there was nothing to do except be on guard for Katie. His ICE team was getting into formation and on the road, and there was nothing he could do from this distance. The sheriff was heading to the old Hochstetler place to comb it for evidence. So now he would wait.

He poured coffee into a cup and chose a seat away from the window but facing the entrance to the area. He sipped the brew, grimacing when it tasted old and bitter on his tongue, and placed the cup on a side table. Determined not to worry about Katie, he retrieved his cell phone and called the sheriff.

Sheriff Moore didn't even answer with *hello*. "You running into more trouble, son?" A smile sounded in his tone.

"No, sir. Just wanted an update."

"We're about two minutes away now. If I find something, I'll be sure to let you know. You sure the fire was out when you drove away?"

"Definitely. You'll see the foam all over the kitchen and doorway."

"No call has come in about a fire, so it must have stayed settled down." There was a pause before the sheriff spoke again. "Hadn't Sarah Miller's brother purchased the place?"

Adam dragged his foot over a spot in the carpet. "Yeah. I told Jed and Sarah that we wouldn't stay with them because we didn't want to bring trouble to their family. Now I'm glad we left there. But what about the damage to the house? It'll need a lot of repair."

"When we're done at the old Hochstetler place, I'll drive by and tell Jed and Sarah what happened."

"It'll be expensive."

"You're probably right. And the Amish don't typically carry homeowner's insurance. They believe they should trust in God rather than an insurance policy. But they'll take care of it. You know how they all come together to raise a barn in a day? Same idea here, except they'll repair and clean up a house."

With thanks to the sheriff, Adam hung up and gulped another bitter swallow of the coffee. It was certainly admirable the way the Amish took care of each other without judgment or bitterness. The repairs to the house would probably be what his grandmother had called a work frolic, and the community would clean it up and set it to rights in no time.

Adam picked up a magazine and absentmindedly flipped through it. Advertisements assaulted him for white teeth, glossy hair and healthy cereal. An article boasted of a decorating makeover of a house on the beach. What was the point of those superficialities, though? He glanced at an orderly walking by and remembered Katie's full lips moving in silent prayer nearly all the way to the hospital. Health and safety were the most important needs in his life right now.

And where was God in all of this trauma and turmoil? Apparently Katie's faith didn't suffer when trouble arose. Why did his? Why did he doubt, especially when bad things happened? Did he really expect that believing in God would just make every moment perfect and serene and wonderful?

Perhaps he should give God another chance. People always wanted a second chance in relationships. His own father had wanted a third and fourth and fifth chance, as well. So why was he so reluctant to give God, Maker of everything, a second chance? His father had made his own choices to leave his faith, and then everything had spiraled down from there, until the drinking was out of control and Adam's brother had also been pulled into that lifestyle. Yet where had that gotten him? In a body bag on the side of the road.

Even Adam had descended into the life of a drunkard for a few years. But all that time on the sofa in a semiconscious state? Opportunities had been lost, until he had managed to pull himself up out of the abyss. He had overcome, mastered the temptation and become a special agent with ICE.

He took one more swallow of the bitter brew and then tossed the cup in the trash. Even with his improved station in life, he still wasn't good enough for the wholesome Amish woman who was now receiving treatment. And he definitely wasn't good enough to join the church. What would God want with someone like him?

But what if he had had the faith of his grandparents? He walked to the window and then returned to his seat, uncomfortable with being still. If he had adopted that level of faith, Amish or not, where would he be right now? His decisions about life and faith had so much depended on someone else through the years. He had let his father and his father's weaknesses determine the trajectory of his own life of faith, or until this point, his life of no faith. Why? Sure, Adam had kicked the drinking habit and made his own choice there. So why couldn't he make his own choice here?

His grandparents, and even an aunt and uncle, had sent him letters through the years, gently urging him to come home. It had been several years since he had seen them, but he still received letters every now and then, inviting him to visit. His grandmother in particular liked to include a description of the meal she would make for him, usually topped off with his favorite pie and homemade whipped cream. If she couldn't get his head to decide to visit, then she appealed to his stomach.

But he couldn't quite make the decision of faith. These last couple of days with Katie had shown him that he wasn't making the difference as an agent that he had thought he would when he'd entered the academy a few years back. And what was he missing of a regular life as he continually ran after the bad guys? But even if he could be accepted among the Amish, wouldn't an Amish life be boring? It didn't seem to count for much contribution to the improvement of life. What can one man working a field do to make the world better? The Amish just hid from the world. His stomach roiled with the agony of a decision. How could he know which sort of life was right and good?

The nurse stepped into the waiting room, and Adam jumped to his feet, closing the distance between them in just a few steps. "How is she?"

"The bleeding has stopped, and she's all stitched up. We also put her on intravenous antibiotics as a precaution, so she'll stay overnight tonight to make sure she rests and that the wound isn't reopened or exacerbated in any way."

"May I see her?" Adam caught himself trying to twist his straw hat and forced himself to stop.

"We're moving her to a room, so you can find her there. Would you like to stay, as well?"

"That's allowed?"

"Sure. I can have them set up the cot in her room."

"Thanks." Adam headed toward the elevator, relief trickling over his shoulders. Katie would be fine, and they had someplace safe to sleep tonight. Perhaps by tomorrow night, all would be well again.

Two floors up, he found Katie sitting up in a white-sheeted bed, wearing a green hospital gown and an IV tube. Her prayer *kapp* was askew, and a few tendrils had escaped and curled on her neck. A weary smile lit her face as he came into the room. "I will be stuck here overnight, but the nurse said I will heal just fine in the end."

"Yeah, that's what she told me, too." He glanced around the room. The recliner had been pulled out into a cot, a white sheet tucked in around its edges.

"*Danki* for saving me. I appreciate your devotion to my safety." An adorable shade of pink crept into her cheeks.

"No problem. Just part of the job."

She looked down, her eyes hidden from him, as the color drained from her face.

When she didn't say anything, he sat on the recliner and laid back. Weariness consumed him. As he drifted off to sleep, he wondered what had made him say that it was just his job to protect her. He raised a hand to rub his eye. Wasn't it true, though? He should forget the whole thing, really. He wasn't good enough for the Amish church or an Amish girl. The past couldn't be erased.

TWELVE

An antiseptic odor tickled Katie's nose, and she lifted a hand to rub away the irritation. But when a pricking sensation caused her forearm to jerk, she immediately stopped that movement. She slid her eyes open to find a white room and Adam dozing nearby.

She inhaled deeply, forcing the memories to return. A nurse had stuck an IV into her arm, telling her it would give her antibiotics to fight infection. It sure hurt, though, and she longed to rub it, although she doubted that would help. Limb by limb, she took inventory of what was wrong and what pained her.

Her left arm was sore from the tetanus shot they had stuck her with yesterday, saying something about it being standard procedure after a wound of that sort. Her leg wasn't too bad, perhaps because the IV had contained both fluids and some sort of painkiller in addition to the antibiotic. A slight headache was coming on, but that could be because of the uncomfortableness of the bed and pillow, as well as her stress over her current condition.

Sunlight streamed in the window, and she stared out

at the cloudless sky. Had they kept her overnight partly because of the IV but also because it would be safer in the hospital? Whether that was true or not, she hated to put this financial burden on the community. She had no health insurance to pay the bill. The cost would be distributed among the members of her church district, and all would contribute. But that was the way of the Amish. Insurance of any kind was forbidden because it was deemed to be a reliance on man and not on *Gott* to provide. Neither did she have a husband with a steady income to help pay a bill that was sure to be large. She glanced around the room at the equipment and monitors. None of this was cheap, for sure and for certain.

Being careful of her tether to the pole that held the IV bag, she stretched, working out the kinks in her back and neck. She did feel somewhat rested. Perhaps she had slept better than the past couple of nights because her protector was right here in the same room.

Adam. She looked over at him on the cot, twisted in the sheet while he still wore his homespun trousers and blue shirt. He wouldn't be much help like that, sound asleep, but perhaps he would wake easily if needed. After his years of training and experience, he was probably a light sleeper.

His hair was mussed from his night of sleep. It was cut so short and so differently from the Amish men she knew. He was certainly different from her husband, who had had blond hair and fair coloring. Adam had a darker tone, with light chestnut hair and brown eyes that seemed to see to the depths of her soul. She continued to stare at him, picturing him with the traditional bowl-style Amish haircut. *Ach*, it didn't take long to determine that he would still be handsome. Maybe even more so.

The door swung open, and a nurse pushed through a rolling cart with a blood-pressure cuff dangling over a hook. Adam woke instantly, sitting up and pulling the sheet away from him. His gaze found her right away, a satisfied smile reaching his eyes when he caught her looking at him. Heat rose up her neck and to her cheeks, and she focused on the nurse, who positioned a cover of some sort on a thermometer and placed it in her ear.

A gentle clamp went on her fingertip, preventing her from straightening her *kapp*. She should have just removed it last night to sleep, but she had been so tired that she had been asleep before she could even think about normal bedtime preparations.

The nurse checked the thermometer and tapped on a computer keyboard on the cart. "Everything checks out, so I think you'll be going home today, but it's up to the doctor."

"Home would be *gut*." Home *would* be *gut*, but she couldn't go there. Where would she go?

"It's nice that your husband could stay overnight with you. Do you have children?"

She had felt flushed already, but now the temperature in the room seemed to rise several degrees. Adam sat behind the nurse, and she looked at him to see him shake his head just enough to seem to signal to her that it wasn't worth the time and trouble to correct the nurse. She would be discharged soon anyway.

"*Jah*, I have twin girls. They are with friends."

"Oh, twins. How fun." She spun to Adam, and Katie smiled to see how quickly he put on a straight face.

"Breakfast will be here soon. Would you like a meal so you can eat with your wife?"

Adam maintained his serious expression as he replied, "Yes, thank you."

"Good. I'll order that, and the doctor will be in when he arrives, but it should be this afternoon, if not sooner." She returned to Katie. "Let me know if your pain meds wear off."

She left quickly, and Katie's abdomen twisted with anxiety at the prospect of leaving the safety of the hospital. Her attackers were out there, looking for her, and that knowledge made her pulse race. She closed her eyes and breathed deeply. Maybe for this brief moment, she could heal.

The breakfast wasn't bad for hospital food, according to Adam. After the trays were removed, Adam spoke to the sheriff again. It seemed that the forensics team couldn't lift a single fingerprint or locate even a few fibers from the Hochstetler place. Whoever the attacker was, he hadn't left a single clue.

As Katie dozed, still waiting for the doctor to arrive with the discharge orders, the door opened. She groggily opened her eyes, expecting the doctor.

"Timothy!"

The tall, light-blond man held a straw hat in his hands and quickly stepped forward to grab one of Katie's hands and kiss her on the cheek. A frown creased his high forehead. "Sister, are you all right?"

"*Jah*, I will be fine. Everything is better now that you are here, safe and in one piece." Katie's heart leapt within her chest at seeing her *bruder* again after more than a month of separation. She nodded to Adam, who had stood and stepped forward. "This is Adam Troyer. He is a special agent and is the reason I am alive."

Adam shook Timothy's hand. "I wouldn't say that, but I'm glad you're here. How'd you manage it?"

"The Amish Taxi is how I got to the hospital. But how I knew that my sister was here is not important." Timothy turned back to Katie, anguish carved across his countenance. "This is all my fault, and I am afraid that my presence here may make things worse. But I could not be a part of that group of criminals any longer. I saw a chance, and I took it."

"*Nein, mein bruder.* All is within *Gott*'s will. I do not understand it, but I accept it."

"It was not *mein* will." Timothy turned his straw hat in his hands, nearly crushing it as he spun it round and round, anxiety radiating from him. "It was forced upon me. I had no choice. They threatened you and the twins if I did not do as they said. Are my nieces all right? Where are Ruth and Rebekah?"

"They are fine and in good care. They are hidden away with some friends."

"Who is in this group of criminals?"

"There are too many people involved, and I have only met those I am forced to deal with. I do not know everybody's names."

Adam leaned in, intense concentration creasing his forehead. "Who is your handler? The man who tells you what to do?"

"I know him as Vic Barthold, but I do not think he is the one in charge. He is what you *Englischers* call a middleman. I am afraid that if he is caught, Katie may still be in danger because there are men above Vic. I do not think that anyone knows Vic's real name or true identity."

Adam looked at the ceiling, deep in thought for a moment as if he were running the name of Vic Barthold through his mental grid. "I can't place the name, but I'll check with my supervisor."

Katie shifted on the bed. "What about the man you hired a couple of months ago? The one who dressed in Amish clothing but did not look or act Amish? Who is he?"

"I do not know his real name. Vic, the man who seemed to be in charge of me, the one who forced me into this smuggling in the first place, sent him to me and said he would be there to watch over me and make sure I did as they wanted. He would even ride with me to deliver the furniture. Vic called him Little Joe. The story Vic told me is that his father is Big Joe, in one of the Amish districts in Holmes County, Ohio, but clearly no one in Indiana knows him. He tried to disguise himself as Amish so that he would be less noticeable."

Adam crossed his arms over his chest and sat on the edge of the bed. "What exactly did they tell you to do?"

Katie struggled hard to maintain the sense of peace she had had earlier that morning. This was the question she had longed to ask her *bruder* for many weeks. And now he was here, about to tell all he knew. Was she ready and prepared to know the truth?

Whether Katie was ready or not, Timothy plunged forward, apparently eager to get it all off his chest and into the hands of a law enforcement officer, who might be able to do something about it. "I make furniture that then is sold to *Englischers* in stores all around the

Midwest. Vic—my handler—stopped me on a routine trip to deliver some finished product to the buyer. He said he had a business proposition for me, and when I refused, he held a gun to me. He already knew about you, Katie, and the girls. He said he would harm you if I did not do as he said. There was nothing else I could do but go along. Now I know too much, and that got you involved."

Katie felt as if her heart would slam out of her chest. The love her *bruder* had for her was overwhelming. He hadn't been doing any of this for himself or because of a pull away from the Amish community. It had all been for her and her daughters.

Timothy drew a deep breath and continued. "I was supposed to begin using a new supplier. There, along with my order of materials, I picked up packages of social security cards and birth certificates. Identity documents I assume were falsified. Then I would hide the papers in panels of the furniture I made. *Ach*, I knew what I was doing was criminal, but I did not know how to make it stop."

"What happened to the furniture after you were done?"

"It was delivered to the different furniture stores across the area. The orders that contained the false documents had fabricated customer names, and then, I assume, men involved in this criminal ring picked up the furniture at that end point, with the documents stashed inside."

Adam stood and walked to the window to look out and then returned to perch on the bed. "That answers a lot of questions that ICE couldn't figure out. We had suspicions of a criminal counterfeiting ring in Northern

Indiana, but we couldn't figure out where those documents went. Bringing in the Amish on their part was a smart strategy. Who's going to suspect an Amish man in a buggy to be involved in criminal activities?"

"*Jah*, exactly." Timothy sat heavily in the chair, his forearms resting on his knees and his head hanging. "And now they have found out that Katie knows something, since she went to my workshop and found that social security card. That means that my cooperation with them will not protect her any longer."

Katie sat forward, her hands flying to her throat. "But I do not know anything. I did not know what that card was for or why it was there. I only wanted to talk to you."

"I know that, but they do not, especially now that you have a law enforcement officer protecting you." He nodded toward Adam. "It looks suspicious to them." He paused. "And you do know something. Did you figure out my note?"

Adam groaned, probably remembering the visit with the bishop.

"*Jah*, but it was not easy to find the right copy of the *Ausbund*."

"So now I am in need of protection, as well." Timothy looked at Adam. "Can we work together to make this all stop?"

Katie bit her lip to try to keep the tears from flowing. Tears of joy that her *bruder* was back, but also tears of sorrow that more danger seemed to lie ahead.

Adam sat up straighter, his mind tingling as he connected the dots. Months of legwork had not yielded the results he was getting with a single conversation with Timothy. Hope surged that this case could finally be closed.

An odd sense of eagerness settled over him as he rubbed the back of his neck. This case felt different. More final. He glanced back at Katie as she straightened the sheet. Did it have anything to do with her? He just wasn't as eager as he usually was to move on to the next case.

He forced himself to focus on Timothy, the man with almost all of the answers. "What does your handler know about the law enforcement that's after him? Has he mentioned any names or agencies or departments?" It was always wise to know what one's opponent knew.

"I do not know how much he knows. He has always been quite careful around me to say only what I need to know to do what he wants me to do. There has been no mention of law enforcement." Timothy crumpled the hat that he still held in both hands. "*Ach*, I am sorry that I cannot be more helpful."

"You're right. That's not very helpful. And we still don't know exactly who is after Katie." Adam scrubbed a hand over his chin. "But it's not your fault. Not at all. These guys are good, and they're careful. I'm sure this Vic Barthold has a dozen different identities at his disposal."

"What more can I do?"

"As soon as Katie's discharged, let's get back to the sheriff's office. I'd like you to tell him what you've told me. He knows the area and the people better than I do, and he's been quite helpful to me. Also, a team of ICE agents are going to rendezvous there, so we can formulate a strategy for tonight. Sound good?"

"I will do whatever I can to be helpful." Timothy grinned at Katie, and she nodded in agreement.

A couple of hours later, after a late lunch, the doctor finally arrived to tell Katie that she could go home. She said *danki* and then just shrugged at Adam. She had no home to return to, but Adam determined not to worry about that until after his meeting with his ICE team. She stepped into the restroom with her clothes and a comb the nurse had loaned her and emerged several minutes later, looking refreshed and put-together. Her sage-green dress accentuated the flashing blue of her eyes, and it looked as if she had combed her hair, straightening the part in the middle and smoothing it back into a bun underneath her prayer *kapp*.

Despite what he had heard about the difficulty of sleeping in a hospital, Adam felt well-rested and even energetic after a full night of sleep and both breakfast and lunch. A renewed hope that the conclusion of the case was near filled him as he led Katie and her brother to the elevator and pushed the down button.

The ride down was quiet, but at the door, Timothy pulled Adam back. "He's here!" His voice was a hoarse and panicked whisper.

His adrenaline spiking instantly, Adam thrust his arms out to hold Katie back from going through the automatic sliding door. All three stepped back in unison, and Adam tilted his head toward a nearby hallway to indicate they should congregate there, away from the windows. "Who's here?"

"Vic. My handler. He is in the driver's seat of that

white cargo van." Timothy and Adam peeked around the corner of the hallway. "The unmarked van just pulling away."

"This isn't good." Adam scraped a hand across his jaw. "They know we're here. The trick will be getting out of the hospital and to the sheriff's office without being seen." He looked at Katie and her brother. "Either of you know a back way out?"

Katie shook her head. "*Nein.* I try to spend as little time as possible at the hospital."

"Okay, we'll figure something out." He grabbed Katie's hand and, with Timothy following, led her down the hallway and around a corner. He peered carefully out every single window they passed, careful not to get so close as to be seen from the outside, but the van was nowhere to be found. The hallway continued to wind around, and with a couple of turns, Adam found an exit door near the back of the building.

A thorough check through the window of the door revealed no threats outside, so Adam pushed the door open and cautiously stepped halfway out to survey further. A narrow street wound past, and he scanned both ways to see if the white cargo van had found them. The alley was vacant, but through a passageway between two other hospital buildings, he could see what looked like a farmer's market.

He quickly turned back to Katie. "What's going on over there?"

Her eyes widened with realization. "*Jah*, of course. It is the Saturday farmer's market held every weekend in the summer."

"As large as a craft festival, since many come to sell

more than just produce. It is in the parking lot of the outdoor shopping mall." Timothy nodded. "A *gut* hiding place."

Still holding Katie's hand, Adam led them across the alley and through the passage to the farmer's market. Tents and awnings and canopies stood sentinel over tables of produce and craft goods, arranged in a way to provide walkways for customers. A few of the vendors had pulled pickup trucks into the fray, to sell sweet corn or melons out of the truck bed, but there was no way to drive a vehicle, let alone a large cargo van, through the market. Adam felt fairly safe that Vic wouldn't come gunning for them with his vehicle as long as they were within the confines of the farmer's market.

"Let's stay close to the vendors and away from the open middle." Adam reluctantly dropped Katie's hand. A glance back confirmed that Katie and Timothy had fallen in behind him in single-file formation, with Timothy protecting Katie from the rear. "And let's wind our way back to my SUV so we can get to the sheriff's office."

As he tried to match the walking speed of the other customers, Adam kept his eye on the perimeter of the market, the closest place Vic could drive. Just when they passed a wagon full of early corn, Adam spied between the booths the white cargo van cruising slowly, the driver hanging his arm out of the window and craning his neck to peer between the booths and vehicles.

"He's here." Adam kept his voice low.

Timothy immediately stepped backward, and Katie and Adam followed, ducking behind the wagon and the tractor that had pulled it. The sweet-and-sticky smell of the ripe corn tickled his nose, and he stifled a sneeze. In between the slats of wood that formed the sides of the wagon, Adam spied the cargo van moving forward. Figuring there was no better way to stay hidden than to keep his opponent in his own crosshairs, he motioned to Katie and Timothy to follow.

Fresh flowers, including some early sunflowers, were set out in five-gallon buckets on rough wooden boards separated by cement blocks to form display shelves. In between the large round flower clusters of some pink hydrangeas, Adam watched the van drive slowly on until it was out of sight. He needed to hurry everyone on to the next vendor so he could keep the van in sight.

The sweet cinnamon aroma of the roasted nuts at the next booth met Adam as he led Katie and Timothy forward. An older man stood behind the high counter made of a couple of two-by-fours, and he nodded at Adam as he walked past, holding out a sample of the nuts. As delicious as they smelled, Adam couldn't afford distraction. Not when lives were on the line. He murmured a *no thanks* and continued on.

At a table of tomatoes and cucumbers, he turned to seek Katie's advice as to which way to go to begin to head back to the hospital parking lot and his Tahoe. "How do we—"

He cut himself off when he saw Katie but not Timothy. His training kicked in to mask his concern, although his heart began a wild thumping beneath his Amish-made blue shirt. Without showing any reaction, he began to scan the many customers walking behind and around them.

"What is the problem?" Katie's voice was low but controlled.

Without ceasing his visual survey of the crowd, he asked, "Where is Timothy?"

"Timothy?" She spun in a complete circle and then grabbed his arm. "Where is he? Did they get him?" Her breath hitched and when breathing resumed, it was shallow and staccato.

"I don't know. Would he have left us voluntarily?"

"No. They got him." Her breath came in short spurts now, and her grip on his arm tightened. "Timothy!" Her voice carried across the crowd, a tinge of panic in it. Several customers turned to look at the loud Amish woman.

"Shh. We can't draw attention to ourselves, or they will find us and not just Timothy." He pried her hand off and grasped her upper arm to steer her past the garden produce and into a walkway created by the divide between two booths.

With no idea how to find Timothy in the crush of customers, Adam was determined to get back to his Tahoe and drive to the sheriff's office. But at the end of the walkway, as they neared the parking lot, a tall, burly, bearded man stepped into their path, blocking their exit.

It was Vic, Timothy's handler, with a malicious sneer snaking across his face.

THIRTEEN

"Gotcha." Vic stepped forward, a menacing grin on his red face.

He was not what Adam was expecting at the end of the walkway, and Adam reeled backward, his hand grasping Katie's arm even more tightly. Katie whimpered, although whether it was from fear of Vic or Adam's pressure on her arm, he could not tell. There wasn't time to figure it out either.

Adam quickly double-stepped them both backward, but there were only a few feet before they would run into the crowd of customers.

"He was at the cabin." Katie's voice was low as she turned her head toward Adam but didn't take her eyes off the man.

"That's right, sister." Vic grabbed her free arm with his meaty hand and pulled. Katie finally broke her staring contest with Vic to toss a frightened glance at Adam.

"Let her go, Vic." Adam refused to let loose of Katie.

"Vic? I don't know anyone by that name." Maliciousness spread across his face like a rash. "Come on, Super Agent, aren't you going to fight for her?"

Vic pulled on her arm, nearly tugging her out of Adam's grasp.

"I have been fighting for her." Adam nearly growled through his clenched teeth. "You haven't gotten her yet."

"Got her now." Vic pulled again as he gruffed out his commands. "Come with me." He pulled back his open button-down shirt to reveal a Glock in a holster.

Whoever this guy really was, he wasn't fooling around with his firepower. Even though Adam still had his piece, he couldn't reach it without calling attention to it. And then Vic would surely take it away.

Katie relaxed her arm in his grip, staring at him until he looked at her. "Adam." She appeared as if she had a mighty struggle to remain calm, which would only be human. But her voice was composed and somehow, with just her tone, she had taken command of the situation, or at least of Adam. "I will go. *Danki* for your protection."

"Not just you, sister." Vic nodded in Adam's direction. "Him, too."

There was nothing more to argue. Vic had the upper hand, and the best Adam could do was to go along and search for an escape.

With his hand still clamped firmly around Katie's upper arm, Vic forced them to cross the parking lot with strict orders to look normal. The white cargo van was idling along the curb, with a second thug sitting behind the wheel. The nondescript vehicle truly was unnoticeable in the parking lot full of other cargo vans and trucks, the vehicles of the vendors at the farmer's market.

With all of the busyness of the market behind them,

the parking lot was surprisingly empty of people. Adam's mind reeled with possible scenarios of escape, but every one of them ended with Katie getting hurt.

Could they make a run for it, hiding behind other vehicles until they got to his Tahoe? But as he scanned the parking lot, it seemed that all of the other vehicles were too far away. They would surely be shot before they could make it ten feet. Besides, Vic still had a hold on Katie's arm.

Could Adam get his weapon out before Vic could react? But Adam's weapon was tucked in a holster at the small of his back. With Vic right next to him, the man would surely be able to retrieve his Glock even before Adam could reach his arm around enough to grab his gun.

Could Adam lunge for Vic and acquire his Glock? But the driver was watching their approach from the van, and professional thugs, as Vic seemed to be, didn't usually travel with only two. There were most likely more standing guard nearby and ready to come to Vic's aid in an instant.

No, escape was impossible.

As Adam mentally ticked off the scenarios, they arrived at the van.

Vic held out his hand to Adam. "I know the Amish don't have phones or weapons, but I'm sure you're packing, Super Agent. Hand over the phone first."

Vic grabbed it when Adam held it out, threw it on the asphalt and ground the heel of his military-style boot into the screen. Even if Adam could still retrieve the phone, it certainly wouldn't work now.

"Now the weapon. Slow and careful."

Adam saw in his peripheral vision that the man be-hind the wheel held his own Glock low, just below the edge of the open window. He retrieved his weapon from the holster and handed it to Vic. With a sneer, Vic took it and stuffed it into a cargo pocket in his pants.

"All right. In you go." Vic pushed around to the back of the cargo van, where he pulled open the doors to reveal Katie's brother. Timothy was handcuffed and guarded by a third thug.

Adam heard Katie suck in her breath at the sight of her brother, but she wisely kept quiet. Talking would come later, and antagonizing Vic would only make things worse for them all.

Katie stepped up into the cargo van, and Adam fol-lowed. His chest clenched at the discouraging thought that they were now hostages. Vic pulled out a second pair of handcuffs and fastened Adam and Katie to-gether. Even as the van doors closed, Adam scanned the parking lot, but there was no one nearby they could holler to for help.

Adam helped Katie get comfortable on the floor of the van and then sat next to her, across from Timothy and their guard. Katie stared at Timothy, her façade of strength cracking a little as she gazed at her brother, who was being held captive in his own set of handcuffs. A tear fell slowly down her cheek, and she lifted her free hand to swipe it away.

"Timothy, what happened?" As Adam asked his question, he watched their guard to see if he would stop them from talking. But the man only glared at him.

"A family with little children stepped right in front of me, and I got separated from you two. Then I was grabbed from behind. I guess I was not careful enough, and the noise of the market covered my words." He shrugged, a gesture of resignation and acceptance of what he probably thought was inevitable. "*Ach*, I am an Amish man. I do not know, like you do, the intricacies of watching out for danger."

The driver nodded to someone Adam couldn't see and then pressed his foot down on the accelerator. The van jerked forward, and Adam ended up leaning into Katie. But when he straightened, Katie continued to lean into him, as if seeking solace and comfort.

"You did nothing wrong." Adam did his best to reassure Timothy. "We're here also, so I didn't do so well watching out for danger either."

Adam was glad they had been able to have a private conversation earlier in the hospital. Would Timothy have been willing, or even allowed, to share all of those necessary details as they rode in the back of the cargo van? It was certainly all information that would be helpful in bringing down this ring of smugglers.

Timothy leaned forward and nodded toward the driver, who was wearing a T-shirt, cargo pants and military-style boots. "That's Little Joe, my Amish employee." Timothy's voice carried a hint of disdain. "When I was forced to switch woodworking suppliers, he came along to make sure I did what I was supposed to with the social security cards and passports that were hidden in the boxes and packages of supplies. He was also the one who supplied the customer names."

Little Joe glanced in the rearview mirror, with a scowl stretched across his face. "That's enough talking." His voice sounded like tires on gravel.

Timothy shrugged again and focused on a spot above Adam's head. Apparently that was all the information he would get.

The van turned to the right and then sped up along what seemed to be a winding road. Since Adam was in Northern Indiana on assignment and didn't know the area well, he couldn't identify many of the roads they might be traveling. Speed and curves and the sound of the tires meant nothing to him. Even if he were allowed to talk to Timothy or Katie, they probably wouldn't be able to name the streets either. Surely each lane, drive and road felt and sounded different in a buggy than in an automobile. He stared out the front windshield, desperate for some idea of their location. But from his position on the floor of the van, all he could see was blue sky with a few clouds and, every now and then, the top of a tree. That wasn't any help at all.

He tried to lift his hand to run it through his hair, a habit he had when he was anxious. But a few inches up, the handcuffs bit into his wrist. Katie whimpered, and Adam whispered an apology as he lowered his hand. If he could whittle, that might help him think. But he hadn't had his pocketknife since he changed into the Amish clothing.

Was an escape possible? He hadn't been able to come up with a plan before they were forced into the van. Discouragement settled heavily on his shoulders as he looked around the inside of the vehicle, their prison.

Could they buy some time to figure out an escape plan by offering to work for Vic and his minions? Maybe a federal special agent and an Amish woman and man would be helpful in their ring? A bump in the road jostled them about, just enough to shake sense into Adam. Their usefulness would not last long, even if they were accepted into the scheme. Eventually they would be eliminated. And why was he trying to kid himself anyway? He would be completely unwilling to join in any criminal activities, and he knew without a doubt that Katie and Timothy would also be unwilling, no matter what the benefits of the deception might be.

God would protect and provide, and Adam knew that Katie would trust in His sovereignty.

"Are you okay?" He bowed his head to whisper to Katie, praying that he wouldn't be noticed by the thug at the wheel.

Katie turned to look at him, her eyes wide, her eyebrows raised. It was a look of forlornness, of weariness, and Adam's heart twisted within his chest at how he had failed her. She simply nodded, but Adam also saw a hope, or at least a peacefulness, that shone through her.

He longed to put his arms about her and absorb that peacefulness. For as long as she would let him.

It made his palms sweat to think of how he had come to care for her in such a short time. Could he imagine a lifetime with her? With every minute that ticked by, the answer became a more resounding *yes*.

He broke the eye contact and looked out the windshield again. His throat felt thick and he swallowed hard with the thought of his desire of a family to call his own, a wife and children. He had no standing, no authority, to want that. A man in his position, with his training and experience, couldn't afford a family. A wife and children would only pull him off course. Loving and raising a family wouldn't make a difference in this evil world anyway.

He may be a failure at his job, as evidenced by his and Katie's current predicament, but his job was what defined him. It gave him a reason to get out of bed in the morning. It assuaged his grief over his father and brother and the way they had wasted their lives, at least for the moments that he was working.

Changing the world for the better was a good goal, but was his job truly accomplishing that? And if it wasn't, then what else was he supposed to do?

Thirst pulled at him. He swallowed hard but it didn't help much. He didn't have much experience trying to gauge speed while riding in a moving vehicle, especially when he couldn't see the road and surroundings. But if he had to guess, he would figure they were moving at about forty miles per hour. The stops and starts had ceased, so they didn't seem to be in town any longer. And the road sounded smooth, like asphalt. But overall, none of that information helped him much.

He glanced back at Katie to see that her eyes were closed and her full lips were moving slightly. Praying again, no doubt. But suddenly that made a lot of sense to Adam. His own resources hadn't helped in this particular case. The way he was choosing to live his own life hadn't brought the fulfillment and satisfaction that he had hoped. But Katie's steady faith in the face of adversity was something he wanted.

It was a faith he needed and a faith that had been ebbing back into his life through the past few days.

Katie, too, was something he needed. He savored the feeling of her arm against him as she leaned into him for comfort and strength. It seemed that every nerve ending on the outside of his arm was acutely aware of her touch. And then a thought struck that forced him upright with the realization of it.

He was falling in love with her.

Katie shifted against him, and he glanced quickly at Timothy across the van, as if the man could read his thoughts about his sister. But Timothy also had his eyes closed as if praying silently. The thug sitting with Timothy made eye contact with Adam, a smirk splayed across his face. Adam quickly looked away, checking the windshield again to see if he could see anything more, but there was nothing new.

What more was there to do but pray? His resources, his strength and his control of the situation were spent. This case had beaten him, and all he had left was God.

He closed his eyes to shut out distraction and began to whisper a prayer. But would the Lord hear him after all his years of trying to live life on his own?

Lord, I need You. With those simple words, a peace Adam had never known seeped through his soul.

Tears dampened Katie's cheeks, but she didn't try to swipe them away this time. The tears, just like her grief, would have to run their course. She glanced at her brother, feeling grateful that he had not left the Amish faith and was now returned to her, but also grieved at all that he had gone through in the past couple of months. Being forced into criminal activity, yet powerless to fight back, must have felt crippling. *Jah*, the Amish were pacifists. But being forced to disobey the law of

God seemed to be an entirely different situation, and one where he had no choice but to comply.

How could *Gott* have allowed this situation? Her brother was a fine, upstanding Amish man, who loved God and obeyed His will.

Another tear fell from her cheek and onto the bodice of her white starched apron. *Ach*, but how could she question the sovereignty of *Gott*?

Gott, help my unbelief!

A lull had fallen over their little group, and she used the silence to try to listen to the sound of the road. Could she hear anything that might help her to know where they were going? *Jah*, she had traveled by bicycle or by horse and buggy over most of the roads in the surrounding countryside, but those modes of transportation only made her feel the bumps and dips even more. Perhaps if she could speed up those bumps and dips, she would have a better chance of determining what road they were on. From her angle, as she sat on the floor of the van, she could tell that evening sunlight was slanting in through the windshield, but she couldn't get much of a view of the outside.

The driver had not stopped for a while and the speed seemed fairly consistent now, so they were probably on a country road. She had been on the interstate a couple of times, a road where the speed had become absolutely dizzying. So she probably wasn't a good judge of how fast they were traveling. But it didn't seem fast enough for the highway. Did that mean they weren't going too far?

But wasn't this line of thinking truly a lesson in futility? If she could figure out their destination, what could she possibly do about it? They were guarded by two men who were armed and in control. Surely this was her darkest moment.

She sighed more heavily than she intended, and Adam leaned farther into her, lending her his strength and comfort. At least she wasn't facing this alone.

If she had decoded Timothy's message correctly— and that seemed to be a big *if*—they could possibly be going to the sawmill. But could a criminal mind even be understood, let alone predicted? They could be going anywhere, like someplace where they would be held for a while or where they would be killed. But there was no way she could ask her *bruder* if she had interpreted his message right. That communication would reveal their knowledge to the thug currently guarding them. And if that thug knew that Katie and Adam and Timothy knew about the meeting, then the criminal gang could be on the lookout for Adam's team coming. That would ruin all possible chances for survival.

Deep in thought, Katie lifted her hand to try to tuck a stray strand of hair back into her prayer *kapp*. But the handcuffs clinking together brought her back to her present surroundings, and she quickly lowered her hand.

"Sorry," she whispered to Adam. The man sitting next to Timothy glared at her but didn't say anything.

She licked her dry lips and wished for a drink. How far from home was she? Her thoughts meandered to her little twins, Ruth and Rebekah, and what they were doing right then. Perhaps eating supper, or depending on what time it was, *redding* up the kitchen after the meal. Jed might be bringing out his big Bible for the after-supper reading of *Gott*'s Word. *Ach*, how she longed to be there.

One thing was for sure and for certain. Sarah and Jed were the truest of friends, and Sarah was the closest thing she had to a sister. Friendship like that was a gift from *Gott*. Her twins may be without her for the moment, but she trusted Sarah and Jed implicitly with her girls. Would she see them again? Ever? Only the Lord knew the answer to that question. Her heart raced at the notion that the end of her life was approaching. It seemed to be a distinct possibility that her twins could be left as orphans.

A thought struck her, shaking clear through to her very soul. The only One who could save anybody was *Gott*. Sure, she had known this for most of her life, but it was only head knowledge. Now that her life was at risk, and it seemed that *Gott* was the only One who could save her physically, the notion that *Gott* was the only One who could save someone spiritually became much more real.

With so much of her efforts and energies directed toward figuring out what had been wrong with her *bruder*, had she actually accomplished anything? Had she made any progress at all? Maybe it was only Jesus who could save him now. Perhaps it was honestly and truly out of her hands.

A shiver coursed through her at the realization. It had been Jesus all along…the only One who could save Timothy. The only One who could save her or Adam or anybody. *Gott* was the One who had saved her and guided her and blessed her, but she hadn't been turning to Him, seeking Him, laying her soul bare as she asked

Him for help with her biggest problem. She had prayed plenty, but it had been prayer as a habit, as something that everyone else in the Amish church did. It was a rote practice. It had not been a real conversation with *Gott*, sprinkled with plenty of quiet in order to listen to His response.

Did Adam have faith? A real faith? She glanced at him, but he seemed lost in thought and didn't return the look. She thought back over the past couple of days. Sometimes it had seemed that he did, but other times she had thought that he didn't. *Gott,* she prayed, *help him to know Your love.*

Did Adam realize that she loved him, as well? Katie gasped and jerked her head up at the revelation. From the corner of her eye, she saw Adam look at her, but she refused to meet his gaze. *Jah*, it was true, although she had not realized it until the quiet moments available for reflection. Yes, he was an *Englischer*. But she was falling in love with him, whether it was wise or not.

The van lurched to a stop, and Little Joe turned from the wheel, a malicious grin on his face. "Everybody out."

Katie's heart beat wildly in her chest at the announcement. What fate waited for them outside the van doors?

FOURTEEN

The sun had just dipped below the trees as the doors at the back of the cargo van opened. Katie peered over Timothy's shoulder for a glimpse of their destination. An eerie glow cast itself over the landscape, and trees loomed large and menacing around the dirt parking lot.

The thug pushed Timothy out first. Katie followed, but she stumbled over the edge of the van and fell toward the ground. Timothy stuck out his bound hands to stop her fall, and she gripped the cold metal of the cuffs, grateful for the help. Adam, still handcuffed to Katie, followed closely behind.

"Move it." With a gun to her back, the man pushed her and Adam around the van and toward a large, dark building.

The sawmill! Katie gasped to see the ominous structure rise up before her. *Jah*, she had interpreted her *bruder*'s message correctly, but that was little comfort as she most likely marched to her death. Of even less comfort was the thought that she would die in the same place as her husband had. She bit her lip to fight back the tears at the irony of it all.

The dark descended rapidly, which meant it was after work hours and no employees would be around to summon help. But it was also Saturday. That meant the mill was closed for the whole next day as well, giving the bad guys a day and a half to carry out their evil deeds at the empty sawmill. There was no hope for employees to return to work to find and rescue them.

Despair gripped her heart like the vise that her *bruder* had in his woodworking shop. Not only had she not succeeded in saving her *bruder*, but her death would orphan her twins. *Jah*, the Amish community would surround her girls with love and provide for their care, but it would not be the same as having a mother and an uncle.

As she stepped slowly across the dirt parking lot, a verse from the Psalms sprang to her mind. *I will bless the Lord at all times: His praise shall continually be in my mouth. Ach, mein Gott, help me to praise You, even here and in these circumstances.*

Her foot landed on the edge of a dip in the packed dirt, and she wobbled, her ankle twisting down into the hole. With his free hand, Adam grabbed her arm to keep her from tumbling to the ground. In her efforts to right herself, a straight pin from her prayer *kapp* pricked her in the scalp. Inspiration struck, and she quickly reached up to straighten her *kapp*.

"I have an idea," she whispered to Adam, tamping down the feel of a smile flitting around her lips.

He continued to stare at the sawmill, his expression serious, but he nodded so slightly that she could barely see it. It was an agreement that in this, their most desperate hour, she should proceed with whatever her idea was.

She suppressed the smile, eager not to draw attention to herself. Staring straight ahead and with what she wanted to be a somber expression, she removed one of the straight pins used to fasten her *kapp* into place. Hopefully it would look to an observer like she was simply adjusting her head covering.

Lowering her hand, she tucked the straight pin into one of the creases in her palm, the cold metal of the pin pressing against her flesh. Perhaps at some point in time, she could pick the lock of the handcuffs. Her mind reeled with what she was planning. Normally on a Saturday evening, she would be at home, finishing her pies and *redding* up her house for visiting on an off Sunday. And yet here, today, she was trying to figure out how to get out of handcuffs and save her life, as well as the life of her *bruder* and a special agent.

She glanced at Adam, his jaw fixed in grim determination. If she had learned anything about him over the past couple of days, she knew from the set of his eyebrows and the wrinkles in his forehead that he was working hard to formulate a plan. She had no idea what all his training and experience encompassed, but surely he would have some idea how to pick the lock of the handcuffs if she couldn't make it work.

The pace was slow and steady, but the sawmill loomed large in front of them anyway. Adam walked close by, but not just because they were still handcuffed together. He cleared his throat softly, and as she looked his way, he cast a reassuring look at her, a smile hidden in the crinkles around his eyes.

"It'll be fine." He kept his voice so low, she could barely hear him.

She nodded in return. "*Jah*, *Gott* is with us."

Little Joe stepped up from behind them and stuck the barrel of his weapon into Adam's side. "No talking."

Adam grunted his defiance and picked up the pace, edging away from the gun, but the thug matched him. The other thug had his weapon on Timothy, and the five of them hurried on toward the sawmill.

The pace was too much for smooth walking though, especially with the unevenness of the ground. Red welts were beginning to mar her skin as the handcuff pulled on her wrist. Subconsciously she began to list the ingredients for a homemade salve that would soothe her skin, if she survived the night. She couldn't rub her wrist either, or hold it to keep the cold metal of the handcuff away from the skin because she was still tightly holding the straight pin in her free hand. Was there a way to transfer the pin to her other hand?

But then they were at the door, the thug right behind her so that his hot breath blew on the back of her neck, and there was no opportunity.

Little Joe stepped around her to grab the door, and the second thug pressed them into the building. Darkness enveloped the structure, and the gloominess of the interior tried to penetrate to her soul. Katie stumbled over the threshold of the door, the pin jabbing into the flesh of her palm. A cry of pain rose to her lips, but she suppressed it so she wouldn't draw attention to herself.

Little Joe grabbed her arm, pulled her up and shoved her farther inside. The second man closed the door behind them with a resounding thud of finality. She shuffled along behind Timothy, trying to see through the gloom and yet afraid to look around. The sweet scent of sawdust overwhelmed her and resurrected vivid memories of the day two years ago when she had been summoned to that same sawmill because her husband had been in an accident.

"Keep moving." The round end of the gun barrel pressed into her shoulder blade as Little Joe growled near her ear.

She forced herself to keep plodding, one foot in front of the other, as she passed the large bay door, where the ambulance had pulled up in an effort to get as close to her husband's body as possible. A muscle jumped under her neck as she thought, as she had a million times since the accident, that her husband never should have taken that part-time job at the mill. Their farm-and-produce income had been enough, but he had wanted to build up some savings as their family grew.

That pregnancy had been an easy one, up until that point. She had had a little morning sickness and had been plenty tired, but after managing twins through infancy and the toddler stage, those symptoms hadn't bothered her that much. Her crochet hook had flown fast through the green-and-white baby blanket, as well as a pair of booties, and even though it was too early for such preparations, her excitement had driven her to retrieve the twins' old baby clothes that had been tucked away in the attic.

On the morning of that fateful day, she had just brought the laundry in from the line and had planned to bake some oatmeal cookies for the twins before she started crocheting a little cap. Miriam from next door, whose husband had a telephone in the barn for his harness business, had come running as Katie stood at the sink, washing the morning's dishes. The message had been grim, and her heart had begun a wild thump even before she had heard the word *accident*. Miriam had volunteered to stay with the twins, who thankfully, at age two, were completely unaware of what was transpiring.

Five long minutes later, the Amish Taxi had pulled up in the lane, though she had not called for it. With hugs from the twins, she had been whisked away by the van, riding in the same vehicle, along the same road, that her husband traveled every day to his job at the mill, since it was too far for horse and buggy. The ride had been silently frantic, and all too soon for her emotions to adjust and her heart to rest, they had arrived at the sawmill, where ambulance lights flashed through the morning sunshine, and huddled groups of workers had cast forlorn looks at her as she approached the entrance.

Inside, the scene had been gruesome. She had learned later that she wasn't supposed to have seen her husband like that. Her husband's boss and the paramedics didn't know she would arrive so soon, and they had not finished their repositioning of him or their cleanup of the area. As soon as they realized she was watching and listening, they rushed her away to an employee lounge and made her sit on a red leather couch.

The miscarriage had struck later that day. While she had lain on a hospital bed on the second floor, being attended by an obstetrician, her husband had lain on a metal slab in the basement morgue, being attended by a coroner.

Now, despite her husband's efforts and good intentions, she had neither savings nor family beyond the twins.

Lost in her memories and dazed by being back at the sawmill, a place she had avoided since her husband had died, Katie stumbled into Adam. The thug had stopped them near several large stacks of boards. Adam grasped her hand, his hand warm and strong over her cold flesh. Her pulse beat through her, threatening to pull her back into a state of being overwhelmed, and she glanced at Timothy. With both of his wrists handcuffed, he was even more limited than she was.

She swallowed hard, forcing the memories and emotions to the back of her mind. Her *bruder* needed her, and she would do her best for him. For Timothy, and for Ruth and Rebekah.

Adam stroked his thumb over the back of her hand, a gesture that was both comforting and thrilling at the same time. And *jah*, she would do her best for Adam as well, and for whatever the future may hold for them.

A tear trickled down Katie's cheek, and Adam's heart twisted within his chest at her obvious anguish. She had told him that her husband had died in an accident at the sawmill, and now here they were. She had been forced to enter the very place where her happy life had ended, and there was nothing Adam could do to protect her from it. It took all his restraint not to slam his fist into the stack of boards or lunge for the closest criminal or make a wild dash for the door with Katie. But none of those actions would help, and would in fact only bring further harm to all three of them.

Self-control, a level head and a compassionate heart were what Katie needed now. God would help him, especially now that Adam had asked Him.

As they had been marched through the sawmill and into the middle of the enormous building, Adam had scoured the structure for exits. There were not many options that he could see, except for the one they had just entered. A few skylights dotted the ceiling, but unless he had a grappling gun, a weapon that could shoot a rope with grappling hooks on one end around the transom and allow them to ascend through the roof, the skylights weren't helpful.

Several windows lined the very top of the walls, near the ceiling. But at a height of at least fifteen feet, those windows couldn't provide an escape. The tiniest bit of setting sun filtered through the opaque glass. It would be completely dark in a matter of minutes. One small light was on, a lamp on a table a few yards away. But considering the time spent driving, they were probably so far out in the country that no one would see it. And who would care anyway? Lots of business owners left lights on in their places of business overnight and through the weekend for security. It was ironic, really. The little light in the dark sawmill should indicate to someone on the outside that someone was inside, yet lights were left on inside a business for security. Adam would have chuckled to himself if he had been capable of finding anything funny at that moment.

He continued his survey of the building.

One entire end of the building looked like a giant garage door, but it was closed and most likely locked. Adam had no doubt that it was secure and would not provide a viable exit. The walls reflected a bit of shine from the low lamplight. They looked to be made of sheet metal, which would mean that he couldn't grab an ax and break through drywall. It also meant that, even if he did have his weapon, which he didn't, it wouldn't be wise to shoot. A bullet could ricochet off many surfaces in that sawmill, and then there would be no telling where it might end up.

Adam didn't know much about milling, but none of the machines in that part of the building looked safe. He was sure that much safety equipment was required to be worn while operating them. One looked like it was designed to skin the bark off logs, and another probably cut them up into boards. Conveyor belts, perhaps for moving the logs and the resulting lumber, stretched back and forth. And almost every bit of equipment contained vicious-looking teeth. They were all machines that would be plenty capable of hurting people. Adam sent up a quick prayer that that was not what this criminal gang had in mind for the three of them.

Timothy cast a forlorn look at Adam as the thug called Little Joe stationed them in front of a stack of what looked like freshly cut boards. Sawdust clung to the top in clumps, and Katie sneezed.

"Stay there," Little Joe ordered them as if they were dogs and then sauntered toward the folding table where Vic huddled with a couple of other men.

After Joe had moved far enough away, Adam looked to Katie and Timothy. "It'll be fine." He wasn't sure exactly what he meant by that, but it seemed he should say something reassuring. Even if their end was death, they would be with the Lord, and that was fine.

"Do you have a plan?" Katie whispered and then sniffled, the sawdust in the air obviously affecting her breathing.

"Not yet, but I'm working on it." He nodded toward the table. "So, Vic is there, as well as the driver of our van and the guy who was in the back with us. Who's the fourth man? Do you know, Timothy?"

Timothy cut his eyes at the foursome, seeming to study the men. "*Nein*, I do not recognize him."

"Maybe he was the advance man and broke into the sawmill before we arrived. There's no way to know for sure." Adam studied the men some more and the stacks of papers spread out over their table. "Any idea what all the paper is? Did Little Joe ever say anything that might indicate what's going on?"

"*Nein*. He was quiet all the time, except for when he was giving me orders."

The papers were most likely counterfeit birth certificates and social security cards that would be handed over tonight to the other part of the counterfeit ring. Why it couldn't pass through the usual channels, such as Timothy, Adam couldn't figure, except perhaps because Timothy wasn't cooperating any longer. Perhaps they had so much material that it was easiest to hand it all over at once. Or maybe they were sure that they could avoid detection by law enforcement.

No matter what the reason, the counterfeiting gang's chances for success increased greatly when they kidnapped Adam. Adam and Katie thought they had determined the location based upon Timothy's secret encoded message. But Adam couldn't lead his team to the location if he was a hostage.

Katie sniffed again. "What should we do?"

Adam's heart broke for her obvious emotional anguish, being held captive in the very place where her husband had been killed. But he prayed that he could save her from that fate and that God would allow him to bring love and security back into her life. He searched the nooks and crannies of his mind for any idea of how to escape, as well as something reassuring to say to the beautiful Amish woman. "Katie—"

"No talking." The thug whom Timothy had called Little Joe had walked up while Adam had been lost in concentration.

Vic stood behind his thug, a sneer stretched across his lips. "Okay, Super Agent, time for a few questions. I need to know what you know."

Adam didn't respond.

"Do you know why we're here? How many ICE agents have you summoned? Do they know where we are? How and when will they be arriving?" Vic held his weapon to Adam's side. "What about that incompetent local sheriff? Will he be joining our party tonight?"

Adam shifted sideways, away from the gun barrel that was jammed into his ribs, but still did not answer. He ground his teeth together as he was forced to admit to himself that he didn't know the answers to those questions. It was better for Katie and Timothy if he didn't assume that help would be coming. It would force him to make a way for their escape.

"That's what I figured." Vic shoved his face up into

Adam's personal space. "Either you don't know any-thing or you're playing tough. Both ways work for me. I'm expecting quite a party here tonight, so even if you are hoping for some reinforcements, I guarantee you they'll be outmanned and outgunned. I'll also get to show you off to my superior. It's quite a badge of honor to capture a federal agent."

Smugness radiated from the man so strongly, it was nearly overwhelming. He obviously believed he had the upper hand. And from all appearances, Adam had to admit that he did. The handcuffs cut into his wrist, and if they were hurting him, he could just imagine how they were hurting Katie and her delicate skin.

Adam clenched his jaw and refused to speak. In his peripheral vision, he could see Katie and her brother watching him, but Adam would not be the first to break the staring contest with Vic. Adam may be in handcuffs, but that didn't mean he was giving up without a fight.

"Got nothing to say?" The man's foul breath punched Adam in the face.

Vic was obviously a man of malicious intent, stop-ping at nothing to achieve his goals. Instead of stopping this counterfeiting ring, what if Adam was forced to join them? What if Adam's goal of making some good come from the senseless deaths of his father and brother was turned against him, and he was put in a position where he had no choice but to join the very thugs he had been working to bring down?

What could be better than an ICE agent hiding their activities, so that they're never found? Would Adam's team get there in time? Or would the team be ambushed before they could even breach the door?

Adam couldn't stand idly by any longer. As he continued to return Vic's stare, he made a fist and tensed the muscles in his free arm. Vic blinked, and in that split second, Adam shoved his elbow up and smashed it into Vic's gun hand.

Shock registered on the man's face. Katie screamed. As Vic's arm jerked upward from the impact, a gunshot rang out across the sawmill.

FIFTEEN

Clammy perspiration popped out on Katie's forehead as she dropped to the floor. The handcuff jerked on her wrist, but that pain was minimal compared to what a gunshot felt like. The wound on her leg throbbed as her full skirt made sawdust billow up from the floor.

"Vic! You all right?" One of the thugs stood up at the table, peering at them.

His gun still in his hand, Vic took a quick step back, out of the reach of Adam. "Think you can fight your way out of here, Super Agent?" A hateful laugh erupted from the men at the table.

Timothy bent down to lend Katie a hand and help her up, sympathy and strength in his eyes. An artery pulsated on Adam's temple, but he still stared at Vic. Apparently no one had been shot, and she quickly found the bullet lodged in a board above their heads and to the side. It seemed that one of the men at the table had fired a warning shot.

"You understand what we're capable of now? This is not a training exercise, Super Agent."

"Vic, need you to look at something." The guys at

the table sorted through a stack of papers, completely nonchalant, as if gunplay were an everyday occurrence for them. Katie's heart grieved within her at the thought of what a desolate and violent life they each must lead.

With one last glare, Vic growled to Adam, "Next time it won't just be a warning." Then he turned on his heel and marched back to his cohorts.

Katie exhaled a long breath that felt like it had been trapped in her lungs all day. She wanted to sag down on the floor and just let it all be over, but the thought of her twins invigorated her to trust *Gott* and trust Adam with her immediate future.

They were alone again and without a guard, at least as alone as they could get with the gang at the table several yards away but still in the same area.

"Katie." Adam kept his voice low and didn't look at her as he continued his watch of the men at the table. "Got the straight pin?"

Ach, the pin! She had forgotten about it completely in the melee. "*Jah*, it is here." As she maneuvered it in her palm in order to hand it to Adam, it jabbed her in the flesh. She winced with the pain.

"Hopefully a team will be here soon. I called them with the location, and when we didn't arrive at the sheriff's office, they should have assumed something went wrong."

Timothy leaned forward. "What about guards posted outside?"

"And are there not more of their gang to arrive?"

"The team's been trained to deal with various scenarios. They'll be careful." Adam took the straight pin from her and began to work on the lock of the handcuffs. "Keep an eye on those guys, and let me know if anyone looks this way."

Katie focused on the men at the table, fighting hard to keep her lip from trembling. Adam lifted the handcuffs that bound them just slightly, and after a few moments of prying the pin into the lock, his cuff came loose. She wanted to sag with relief at their small victory, but she forced herself to stay upright and keep watch.

As Adam began to work on her cuff, Vic looked up from his papers and stared directly at her.

"Adam," Katie whispered out of the corner of her mouth. "He is looking."

Katie felt Adam stand upright, his arms dangling at his side, probably trying to look as if nothing had happened.

Vic looked back at the documents, seemingly satisfied, and Adam resumed his lock picking. The cuff bit into her wrist as Adam worked at it, and a few moments later her cuff also came loose.

But then Vic looked up again, and although Adam jolted back to position, Vic left the table and sauntered in their direction.

"Look normal. Be cool." Adam whispered encouragement to her.

Katie grasped the handcuff and, with her wrist nearly twisted backward, struggled to hold it in place to make it look as if it were still locked around her wrist. Adam seemed to be doing the same with his cuff, since it did not dangle. Would he try to overtake Vic now that they were free from the handcuffs? Was that his escape plan?

But Vic didn't notice the handcuffs. He just walked

up to Adam and sneered at him, as if he were quite satisfied with the presence of his hostages. Katie felt all her muscles tense as she waited to see what Adam would do. But he only returned the stare, and a few moments later, Vic turned back to the table.

Katie forced her shoulders to relax as she snuck a glance at Adam. His jaw seemed softer now, not quite so grim. Did she dare to hope that he was trusting *Gott* a little bit more with their situation? Was he softening to a renewal of his faith? Gratitude flooded her that he hadn't tried to overtake Vic. Of course Adam was a smart man, and he surely had factored into his thinking the fact that the men at the table had all the weapons. If it had been revealed that they were free, the others at the table would certainly have opened fire. All would have been lost.

When the men seemed engrossed in their stacks of paper again, Adam angled slightly toward Timothy to work on his handcuffs. Katie watched her brother's face as he maintained a vigil for anyone approaching. His expression was somber and unrevealing, like she had seen many times before. But as his sister, she knew the heart for *Gott* that beat inside him, as well as the trust of *Gott* that gave him peace. Memories from the calm they had shared before the current storm, before the counterfeiters had sunk their criminal claws into their family, washed over her. Life had been normal, predictable. Even comfortable, or at least as comfortable as it could be after the loss of a husband. And despite the loneliness she had endured, and in fact continued to endure as a widow, she would return to that time in an instant, that time where none of this had happened.

As he maneuvered to reach the lock better, Adam's shoulder bumped hers. She looked at his face, his growth of stubble because he hadn't even taken the time to shave in his vigilant protection of her, the intelligence that shone from his light brown eyes, the handsomeness in the strength of his jaw.

Ach, would she return to the life she had had before this danger? Suddenly she did not know for sure and for certain that she would. That was before Adam had come into her life. Was he not worth knowing—and loving— even if this peril was the price she had to pay? She had already admitted to herself that she was falling in love with him. Was there any hope, any prayer, that they might survive and that he might decide that the Amish life was for him?

Before a petition to *Gott* could spring to her lips, Adam's husky voice reached her. "Let's go."

Had Timothy been freed from his handcuffs while she had been lost in thought? She spun to her brother, and he simply nodded toward the door they had come in through.

Adam grabbed her hand and tugged her along. At first they sidestepped slowly, trying not to be noticed. But when Little Joe looked up, his eyes widened as he realized their escape plan. His weapon was out of the holster in a split second, and his movement caused the other thugs to stand in a rush. In an instant, all guns were pointed at them.

"Run!" Adam pulled on Katie, and Timothy followed closely behind. Her leg pained her, but she gritted her teeth and forced herself to put her full weight on it in order to keep up with Adam. She didn't want to be the one to keep them from getting away.

As they passed the stacks of boards, the exit door came into sight. But a series of loud pops suddenly filled the mill. Immediately it felt as if her leg were on fire, and her flesh seared. She stumbled on the cement floor, a cry escaping as pain engulfed her. Had her leg been hit again? The entire limb burned as the floor rushed up to meet her.

"Adam!" His name was the only thought in her mind.

She landed on the cold cement, her shoulder hitting first. The mill swirled around her consciousness. Adam's face appeared above hers, and she battled to focus on it. But the spinning only increased, a dizzying swirling and whirling, until darkness overtook her.

"Katie!" Her name sprung to Adam's lips. As if he were caught in quicksand, unable to move, he watched her go down, her hand involuntarily clutching her leg, where the bullet had hit.

Adrenaline pulsed through him. He lunged for her, to catch her, to keep her conscious, to do something or anything to save her life, when a searing agony ripped through his biceps. In that nanosecond, a thousand thoughts flitted through his mind. He would have to turn away from Katie, ignoring her and her need of him, and face Vic. Otherwise he would be shot dead. If he were killed, he could no longer be a help to Katie or her brother. At least by obeying the thug with the gun, there was still a chance, however slight, to survive and to get Katie help before it was too late.

He turned to find the source of his pain and saw Vic

pointing his weapon directly at him. Behind him, the other three had their guns drawn and pointed at the would-be escapees.

Out of the corner of his eye, Adam saw that Timothy's face was contorted with anguish as he stole glances at his sister, his only family left, lying unconscious on the floor. Unable to stand still and do nothing any longer, Timothy moved toward Katie.

Vic took a step forward. "Don't move, boy." His voice growled like a threatened dog. "You stay put, and I'll deal with you in a minute."

Adam shook his head slightly at Timothy, cutting his eyes in the direction of where Timothy was standing before he moved. Would he get the message that he should return to his position? When he didn't move, Adam ventured to speak, despite the risk of further angering Vic. "Best to obey the man's orders, Timothy."

A sneer snaked across Vic's lips. "Yes, Timothy." His tone was laced with malice. "It's best to obey me."

As Timothy inched back, forcing his gaze from Katie, Adam tried to assess Katie's injury from what he could see in his peripheral vision. He couldn't see much blood coming from her leg wound, and there was no puddle under her. So he dismissed, tentatively, the possibility that she could bleed out. But if she was in shock, if that was the reason for her unconsciousness, then she would need treatment fast. Her face looked pale, but was her skin clammy? Did she have a rapid pulse? If he could just examine her, lift an eyelid to see if her pupils were dilated, he could tell more about her condition. She needed an ambulance, direct pressure on her wound to stop any bleeding, elevation of her legs.

And did she hit her head on the floor? He had no way to tell from that distance. At least Vic seemed to have forgotten about her. That increased her chance of survival.

But for now he was stuck where he was until Vic looked away. Or shot him again.

"What's your plan here, Vic?" Adam shrugged. Why not just ask a direct question? "Are you going to let her die?" He gestured toward Katie, sneaking another glance at her.

"I might. She's not necessary anyway." Vic leveled the weapon at Adam. "You know what? You're expendable, as well."

Adam refused to close his eyes in anticipation of the gunshot. He wanted to be conscious and alert to his very last moment.

One of the guys still at the table hollered, interrupting their staring contest. "Vic, got a call."

Vic lowered his weapon slightly and half turned back, rolling his eyes at the interruption. "Can't you deal with it?"

With Vic distracted, Adam grabbed the opportunity to shuffle backward toward the stack of boards nearby. He had noticed on the way in that there seemed to be boards stacked everywhere with different levels of sawdust coating them. That fact hadn't seemed important at the time, but now inspiration struck him. One inch back led to another inch back as Vic and his minions argued about the phone call and who would do what. Timothy just looked at him wide-eyed and held his ground as if he knew that he should stay still to reduce the chance of Vic noticing them.

With just a few inches left between him and the stack of boards, Adam reached back, moving as slowly as an inchworm. He grabbed a handful of sawdust from the top of the stack and clenched it in his fist. The more he could manage, the better his chances of success. Immobilizing Vic could buy them the time needed for an escape.

The bickering ceased, and Vic turned his attention back to Adam, not seeming to notice Adam's fist clenched at his side or that he had edged backward. Vic stepped forward, his weapon pointed again at Adam's heart, and sneered in Adam's face, a malicious smile that showed a couple of yellowed teeth and emitted his foul breath. "This is it. Say goodbye."

Adam brought his hand up to his hip. "That's right. Goodbye."

Confusion darted across Vic's face. Adam seized that moment to bring his hand up, unclench his fist and blow the sawdust into Vic's face.

The cloud hovered around Vic, clinging to his hair, his eyelashes, his cheeks. He stumbled backward, immediately dropping his weapon and grabbing at his eyes as if he could claw out the minuscule bits of wood. Vic howled with pain.

A vicious-looking tool lay on top of a nearby stack. Adam grasped the solid-wood handle, leaving the large metal hook swinging on the underside. Despite his wound, adrenaline surged, and his arms tingled with the anticipation of swinging the weapon and defending himself. Old habits usually died hard, and it was in his training to fight to defend those who needed his protection, including the woman he loved.

Yet his fingers loosened their grip on the hook as a new and unusual sensation of calm soaked through him. He honestly didn't want to harm the man. He didn't want to do it. But was his faith rebuilt? Was he ready to adopt the Amish idea of peacefulness with his fellow man and pacifism? *Jah*, definitely so.

Vic clawed at his eyes, groaning more loudly and attracting the attention of his cohorts in crime. As the other brutes approached, weapons at the ready, loud shouts sounded from the door as more men entered.

Suddenly they were surrounded.

SIXTEEN

"**D**rop your weapons!"

As men in tactical gear streamed in around him from every corner of the building, Adam recognized many faces as those of his own team, as well as several more men sent as reinforcements.

Vic's weapon had already been dropped, but Little Joe and the other thugs behind him quickly lowered their guns, letting them clatter to the cement floor. Their smirks turned to grimaces as they raised their hands in defeat.

Adam slowly unclenched his fists as his heart rate began to slow to a more normal pace.

"Troyer, we got them on the outside, too. Good work, son." Sheriff Moore followed the others in as another ICE agent took up a position to protect the door.

It was over. There wasn't success with every case, but this one was ending well. Adam closed his eyes as tension flowed from his body.

"Can we get some help over here, please?" Timothy rushed to Katie's side and dropped to his knees.

His call drew Adam's attention. It had barely been a couple of seconds since the team had arrived, but his heart raced anew with the sight of Katie on the ground. Her chest still rose and fell with breath as two paramedics arrived with a stretcher. He breathed easier to see that sign of life. But as he stepped toward her, eager to see to her care and well-being, the sheriff caught his arm.

"Your team needs you." He nodded toward the folding table, where a couple of special agents were looking through Vic's documents.

Adam looked at his fellow agents and then back at Katie as she was lifted onto the gurney. Timothy held her hand as the paramedics began their assessment. Adam's abdomen twisted within him. Shouldn't *he* be the one holding her hand?

"Need to do your job first, son. Leave the woman to her brother." The sheriff's voice was low but firm with his admonishment.

His brow pulled down in concentration, Adam watched a paramedic elevate Katie's feet with a pillow and cover her with an emergency blanket. The sheriff was right. Adam needed to do his duty and complete his mission. Katie was being cared for, and Adam's first obligation was to ICE and his team.

But all he wanted in that moment was to be by her side. He wanted to forget about the job and just be with her, secure her health and safety, comfort her as she returned to consciousness.

He forced himself to turn away from her and trudge

toward his team as they began to process evidence. But one thought remained in the back of his mind.

What job could he do in which he wouldn't have to leave her again?

Katie's eyelashes fluttered against her cheeks like butterfly wings on her skin. A dull throb began to pulse in her head with the effort it seemed to take to open her eyelids. She forced them open a fraction of an inch, but bright light made her drop them closed again. With a wiggle of her hands, she tested the strength of her wrists. She tried to lift a hand to brush some hair off her forehead, but she quickly dropped it to the bed again for lack of strength. As she began a physical inventory of aches and pains, the wiggle of her feet brought a sudden jolt of pain to her leg.

Her gunshot wound. It all came back in a rush. She wiggled her wrists again to find that the handcuffs were gone. The mattress was soft beneath her, so she wasn't on the hard floor of the sawmill any longer. A soft blanket comforted her. Her heart leapt within her as she remembered everything that had happened and realized she was safe.

Katie steeled her nerves for the harsh white light. Slowly she forced her eyes open once more. A white ceiling overhead came into view, although it was fuzzy. She cut her eyes to the side, and a face appeared in her vision.

"Timothy." Her throat scratched as she wobbled out the name.

Her brother grasped her hand. "Do not move. I think you will hurt less if you stay still."

"Ambulance?" She looked around to see small cabinets of supplies and a kind-looking woman on her other side.

"*Jah*, you are in the ambulance. And you will be fine…eventually."

"Mrs. Schwartz? Or may I call you Katie?" The paramedic smiled at her with a comforting warmth and held a cup with a bendable straw toward her.

Katie sipped the cool water and let it soothe her throat before she answered. "*Jah*, call me Katie."

The paramedic set the cup on a small counter. "How do you feel?"

"Like I have been through the wringer."

The woman removed her protective glasses. "A bullet grazed your leg and reopened your wound, so you probably feel some aching. I've given you something for your pain." She gestured toward an intravenous bag hanging from the ceiling of the vehicle. "You had passed out from shock before we arrived, but I believe you'll have a full recovery."

"*Danki* for taking care of me." Katie also appreciated that the paramedic spoke in language she could understand, not her medical jargon.

"Thank your brother. He's stayed by your side the entire time."

She rolled her head to look back at Timothy. "Is it all over, then?"

He smiled at her. "*Jah*, the bad men are all in custody. There are so many law enforcement officers in there, it makes my head spin. *Ach*, it is an evil world we live in."

"There has always been evil, *mein bruder*, even back to the Garden of Eden. Please. We are together again. Let us dwell on that right now." She squeezed his hand, savoring his presence.

"But this is all my fault. I am why you became involved in this mess. I am why you are in this ambulance right now." He cast his gaze down at the floor.

"*Nein*, it is not your fault. It was out of your control. Besides, it is done now, for sure and for certain." Tears trickled from the corners of her eyes and dropped to the sheet that covered the cot.

It thrilled her that Timothy was safe and out of danger now, and there with her. But what about Adam? Her heart thumped and bumped as she looked about for him from her limited view on the gurney. Did he survive? Where was he? Was he alive and well or in a body bag?

Tightening her abdominal muscles, she strained to sit up, the line from the IV bag pulling on her arm.

The paramedic quickly and gently pushed her back down. "You need to lie still a bit longer. And soon we'll transport you to the hospital. You're going this time. No arguments."

The hospital? She couldn't, not without finding out about Adam. "But what about…? I mean, where is…" She slumped back into the cot and picked at the blanket that covered her. Was she betraying her *bruder*, and even her Amish faith, with her concern for Adam? Adam was an *Englischer*. *Jah*, over the past few days he had seemed to soften toward the Amish. Had even kissed her, a *wunderbar* kiss that had *ferhoodled* her, for sure and for certain. But now that the danger was done, would he change his mind? Were his words of care and concern only uttered because of the danger of the moment?

The paramedic tapped her arm, and Katie looked up into her warm and understanding gaze. The woman inclined her head toward the open back door. Adam stood there, gazing at her, his look intense and concentrated.

And suddenly, with his presence, all was right with her world.

Timothy cleared his throat next to Katie and rose from his stool. "I will go see what more I can do for the sheriff."

After he squeezed through the door, Timothy shook Adam's hand. "*Danki.* We would never have survived this without your help and protection. *Danki* especially for taking care of Katie." Her brother's voice broke as he said her name.

As Timothy walked back toward the sawmill, Adam hopped into the ambulance with her.

Tears pooled in her eyes, but she did not care. This man had seen her at her worst and had still taken care of her. "You are hurt?"

"Not really. Just a scratch. I was treated in a second ambulance, and it'll be fine." His gaze relaxed, and little lines crinkled at the edges of his soft brown eyes. "I wanted to check on you."

Katie glanced back at the paramedic to see if she would answer, but the woman had turned her back on them and seemed to be busy organizing a small cabinet. "I am told that I will be fine, but I have to go to the hospital this time."

"Yes, and I'll go with you." With no apparent thought for the presence of the paramedic, Adam drew her into his arms, being mindful of the IV. "I know we've only spent a few days together, and the circumstances have been extreme."

"Jah." The interior of the ambulance swirled around her, but it was not a medical condition this time. Any lingering sense of cold she had had disappeared with his arms around her.

"But I think you should know that I'm falling in love with you."

Even with a small bandage on her forehead, her dark blond hair mussed and her prayer *kapp* askew, she was beautiful. Adam could look at her face for the rest of his life.

Whoa, really?

He scrubbed a hand through his hair, not caring that that nervous gesture would dishevel him even more. This lovely creature had been with him in the most dire of circumstances in the past few days, and she had seen him through thick and thin.

Yes, really.

It only took a moment of remembrance of the strength that she had exhibited, her loving interactions with her twins and her care for him even when she had been in danger. He knew.

How could he voice those emotions? He wasn't sure he had the strength or the presence of mind just then. A lot had happened over the past days that he would need to analyze and process. But there was something he could say.

Should he ask the paramedic to leave? But did it matter if she had heard? It was no secret, certainly not now, that he cared for this lovely Amish woman. And after that night's pulse-racing danger and the scare of losing Katie, he was certain. "Katie, this might seem sudden to you. But God has been at work in me, and I want to join the Amish church. To slow down. To worship and praise God within the community of believers." He wanted to wake up every morning with her. To raise a family of a dozen children. To get his hands dirty growing crops or raising chickens or whatever it was he would do to support a family. He could whittle. Maybe he could develop those woodworking skills into an occupation.

Katie looked down at the blanket, sending his heart into a tailspin. What if she didn't return his affection, his love? What if he had to leave that ambulance alone and without hope? Would he be able to return to the life he had considered normal just a few short days ago?

"I'm sorry it isn't romantic." His voice was husky, but he couldn't help the emotion swelling within him. A thousand times it had been on his lips to tell her that he was falling in love with her. Why hadn't he? And now, would it be too late?

She looked up at him, her dark blue eyes luminous and—could he dare to hope?—expectant.

In her silence, the clink and clatter of bins and supplies sounded around them. He didn't care. He wasn't a man of many words, but those particular words said everything he was trying to communicate, so he repeated them. "I love God, and I love you."

Slowly, like the sun sending out its first rays in the morning to warm the earth, a smile radiated across her face. "Wherever we are together, that is where I want to be. I love you, too, Adam. But please, no more ambulances."

EPILOGUE

Crisp, colorful leaves had crunched under Katie's feet that morning as she and the twins left the house for the service on Preaching Sunday. The autumn was becoming so chilly that she would soon have to pull their black winter capes out of the attic.

Now warmth and wonderful fall aromas surrounded her as she stood in the serving line at Jed and Sarah's house, dishing out pieces of pie as the men passed by. Adam stepped through, accepting a piece of raspberry pie and looking handsome in his blue shirt and homespun pants. He smiled at her with a mischievous look twinkling in his eyes.

His baptism into the Amish church had been a beautiful event, and Katie had had to dab at her eyes several times. It was a *wunderbar* thing when a person turned from a focus on the world and sought a focus on the Lord, accepting a life of simplicity in communion with other like-minded believers.

After the men were seated at long tables outside, an arrangement that wouldn't last too much longer as the days turned chillier, the women filled their plates. Katie was halfway through her piece of pineapple upside-down cake and almost ready to jump up to refill coffee cups when Adam snuck up behind her.

"May I steal you away for a few minutes?" His voice was low in her ear and tickled the back of her neck.

She nodded and stood. The other women at the table smiled at Adam and then at her and then back at Adam. These past few months, Adam had taken baptismal classes, become better acquainted with the men in the community, met with the bishop and spent plenty of time with her. He had also been putting his whittling skills to good use by working closely with Timothy to learn woodworking. Soon he would make and sell Amish furniture. The district had accepted him without hesitation and had not failed to notice the growing romance between them.

Adam led her past the tables of church members eating. Girls were jumping rope in the lane, and some bare-footed boys were throwing a ball back and forth. Timothy waved in greeting from where he stood, talking to the bishop in what looked to be an easy and casual conversation. Vibrant mums of orange and yellow and purple graced the flower beds, the color so vivid that it seemed like the mums were competing with the oranges and reds and golds of the surrounding trees. Leaves crunched under their boots as they meandered toward the barn.

They left the crowd behind, and Adam held the branches of a weeping willow to the side to allow Katie to pass ahead of him into the enclosed space inside the drooping leaves. As the sun shone through the leaves, a golden glow surrounded them.

She leaned against the tree's trunk. "It was a beautiful service, *jah*?"

"Jah." He smiled at his own use of the Pennsylvania German. "It is *wunderbar* to sing from the *Ausbund* and use it as it is intended. Not for decoding a secret message."

"Definitely." She returned the smile. "And you are pleased with your decision to join the Amish church?"

"I always thought the only way I could change the world was to catch the bad guys and put evil behind bars. But you helped me to see that I can have an impact on the world from inside the Amish church, by raising a good family and keeping the simple ways."

"Jah, family is important." Through the branches, she glimpsed the green shirt of her brother. "That is why I had to get *mein bruder* back."

"He seems quite content to be back in the fold, and his business is going well. I also saw him making eyes at the young lady serving the casseroles this afternoon."

Katie had noticed that, as well. Her brother would probably be courting soon, now that life was getting back to normal. "What about the trial coming up?"

"Well, Vic and Little Joe and the others are still behind bars, and they'll stay there until they are tried. So all is safe and well. Considering the amount of evidence against them, I don't doubt they will be convicted. The only real question is how long they'll serve."

"Will you attend the trial? What did the bishop say?" Katie hugged her arms around her middle at the idea of Adam in the courtroom. The Amish did not, as a rule, become involved in legal proceedings, but perhaps there wasn't any other option in this situation.

"I'll have to testify since I'm an eyewitness. The bishop has given me permission to don my ICE uniform one more time for the trial. If I'm there testifying in my capacity as an ICE agent during those events, then the lawyer and jury will expect me to dress the part. I don't want to cast doubt on my testimony or endanger the chances of a proper sentence by appearing in my Amish clothes."

"*Jah*, I understand that."

"That's over. Let's not talk about those events anymore." The twinkle reappeared in his light brown eyes, the gold specks nearly shining. He smiled wide and ran his hands down her arms, grasping both hands in his.

Katie's heart beat harder as she let him hold her hands. It seemed there was only one other thing he might want to talk about, considering the nervousness mixed with anticipation that spread across his smile, but she did not want to assume what he was feeling and thinking.

He leaned forward and kissed her on the forehead. "I don't have a lot to offer. I'm still learning the business of making furniture. But I'm a hard worker, and I trust in *Gott* to provide and answer prayer. What I can give you is my love, my affection, my devotion, for as long as we both shall live."

Her throat tightened at those words, and tears of joy stung her eyes. *As long as we both shall live?*

Adam squeezed her hands. "Katie, will you marry me?"

A tear trickled down her cheek unbidden. "*Jah*, I will. For sure and for certain."

He leaned in again, but this time he touched his lips

to hers, a sealing of their commitment to each other. His lips were soft and warm, and she wanted him to linger there forever.

With a shout, the twins parted the branches and ran in to grab Katie's legs. Adam pulled back but not before he whispered in her ear, "We'll continue this later."

Her heart thrilled at the promise. The twins each reached their arms around her waist, and Adam pulled them all into his embrace. Another tear of joy escaped, and her heart felt as if it would burst. *Gott* was blessing her with family again.

* * * * *

If you enjoyed this story, look for
Amish Country Amnesia
by Meghan Carver
from Love Inspired Suspense.

Dear Reader,

Thank you for reading! Adam certainly had a struggle, didn't he? As a child, his family life was torn apart by evil, and he grew up thinking he should never hope for a family because he needed to fight the evil. He thought a family would distract him from that goal. Yet he learned that devoting himself to a family was a fight against evil as well.

Katie struggled with control as so many of us do. Her prayers had become habitual, not a time of true communion with *Gott*. But in the search for her brother, she realized that *Gott* is the One who is ultimately in control and she needed to trust Him more. By the time she reached the sawmill, she was ready to admit that many things were out of her power and she needed to pray and leave it in *Gott*'s hands. He always comes through!

I would be honored to hear from you. You can visit my website at www.MeghanCarver.com, where you can sign up for my author newsletter, or email me at MeghanCCarver@gmail.com. If you're on Facebook, I'd like to be your friend at Facebook.com/MeghanCarverAuthor. If you wish to write the Amish way, on good, old-fashioned stationery, you can send it to me c/o Love Inspired Books, 195 Broadway, 24th Floor, New York, NY 10007.

Many blessings to you,
Meghan Carver

Get 4 FREE REWARDS!

We'll send you 2 FREE Books plus 2 FREE Mystery Gifts.

Love Inspired® Suspense books feature Christian characters facing challenges to their faith... and lives.

FREE Value Over **$20**

YES! Please send me 2 FREE Love Inspired® Suspense novels and my 2 FREE mystery gifts (gifts are worth about $10 retail). After receiving them, if I don't wish to receive any more books, I can return the shipping statement marked "cancel." If I don't cancel, I will receive 4 brand-new novels every month and be billed just $5.24 each for the regular-print edition or $5.74 each for the larger-print edition in the U.S., or $5.74 each for the regular-print edition or $6.24 each for the larger-print edition in Canada. That's a savings of at least 13% off the cover price. It's quite a bargain! Shipping and handling is just 50¢ per book in the U.S. and 75¢ per book in Canada.* I understand that accepting the 2 free books and gifts places me under no obligation to buy anything. I can always return a shipment and cancel at any time. The free books and gifts are mine to keep no matter what I decide.

Choose one: ☐ **Love Inspired® Suspense Regular-Print** (153/353 IDN GMY5) ☐ **Love Inspired® Suspense Larger-Print** (107/307 IDN GMY5)

Name (please print)

Address   Apt. #

City   State/Province   Zip/Postal Code

Mail to the **Reader Service:**
IN U.S.A.: P.O. Box 1341, Buffalo, NY 14240-8531
IN CANADA: P.O. Box 603, Fort Erie, Ontario L2A 5X3

Want to try 2 free books from another series? Call 1-800-873-8635 or visit www.ReaderService.com.

LIS19R2

SPECIAL EXCERPT FROM

HQN™

In the wake of his estranged wife's murder, widower
Michael Forster returns to the Amish community
he'd left as a teen, seeking a fresh start for himself
and his daughter, Allie, but the past is determined
to follow him...

Read on for a sneak peak at
Amish Outsider *by Marta Perry,*
the first book in the new River Haven series,
available July 2019 from HQN Books.

Cathy looked up again at Michael, to find him watching
his child with a look compounded of love, protectiveness
and bafflement. Maybe he wasn't finding it easy to be a
single dad. Her heart twisted with pity, and she longed to
reassure him.

"If she gets upset—" he began.

"Please don't worry about it. She'll be fine. If there are
any problems, I'll send someone to fetch you. You're at
Verna's house, ain't so?"

He nodded, giving her a bleak look. "News travels
fast."

"It's a small town." If he remembered anything about
River Haven, he ought to remember that.

"Yes. And people have long memories."

There didn't seem to be any answer she could make.

"I'll be here to pick up Allie at three o'clock. Don't let her leave with anyone else." It was an order, and he followed it by striding out the door.

Michael had gone, but he'd left a turbulence in the air. Or maybe the turbulence was only in her.

She'd heard all the stories about him, and her instinctive reaction had been to believe him innocent. How could someone who'd been raised here, who'd grown up nourished on simple Amish values of faith and family, honesty and humility, possibly have done such a thing?

Now she'd encountered him for herself, and she didn't know what to believe. She had expected to have a sense of the familiarity that linked Amish to Amish. But that hadn't happened. He seemed foreign to her, as if there was no point at which their lives could touch.

Collecting herself, she walked between the rows of desks to the front of the room and picked up the Bible that lay open on her desk, ready for the morning reading. Her gaze lit on Allie, who was watching her with a sort of shy hope in her face.

Cathy's heart warmed, and she smiled. If she looked for a point where their lives touched, it was here in the form of a small child who needed her.

Don't miss
Amish Outsider *by Marta Perry,*
available July 2019 wherever HQN Books
and ebooks are sold.

www.Harlequin.com

Looking for inspiration in tales
of hope, faith and heartfelt romance?

Check out **Love Inspired**® and
Love Inspired® **Suspense** books!

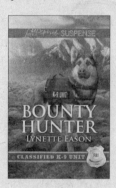

New books available every month!

CONNECT WITH US AT:

Facebook.com/groups/HarlequinConnection

Facebook.com/HarlequinBooks

Twitter.com/HarlequinBooks

Instagram.com/HarlequinBooks

Pinterest.com/HarlequinBooks

ReaderService.com

Love Inspired®

LIGENRE2018R2

Inspirational Romance to Warm Your Heart and Soul

Join our social communities to connect with other readers who share your love!

Sign up for the Love Inspired newsletter at **www.LoveInspired.com** to be the first to find out about upcoming titles, special promotions and exclusive content.

CONNECT WITH US AT:

Facebook.com/groups/HarlequinConnection

 Facebook.com/LoveInspiredBooks

 Twitter.com/LoveInspiredBks